YET ANOTHER SLICE OF FEAR

...Short Stories of Suspense and Terror

BY ANDREW ALLEN SMITH

Yet Another Slice of Fear

Short Stories of Suspense and Terror

By Andrew Allen Smith

Print ISBN: 978-1-7373373-8-6

eBook ISBN: 978-1-7373373-9-3

LOC: On File

For more information, please go to AndrewAllenSmith.com

Dedication

I considered dedicating this book to a lot of people. When you write a book, you often get lost in that idea that someone special is out there that will see their name in a dedication and melt into a festering puddle of goo. With Horror/Thriller stories, it is not the same as they go, "ick, why would you do that to me?" As I ponder, I consider the possibility of dedicating this book to Dana. After all, I threw her into the bottom of a lake and worse in this volume. I also considered dedicating this book to several authors who have been inspiring along the way, to an editor, or to someone who inspires me.

I could also dedicate this book to Alice Krige, who is one of the nicest people I have ever met, or to her husband, who is absolutely amazing as well.

Instead, I would like to dedicate this book to you. Select yourself as the most important person in this book. If you met me, I probably asked what scared you and made a show out of that. If you are a reader who is having a little fun, and maybe you're seeing a little bit inside my less-than-normal. Won't that be swell?

Hats off to you and thanks for reading!

Authors Rant

I find myself in an interesting place. I've always loved writing short stories and have hundreds of complete and partial stories written about just about everything. By far, my biggest focus has always been suspense and horror. I've tried to share that with people, and sometimes, I'm even successful. The trick is finding the right formula.

Fear is a very unique emotion, and at festivals this year, I asked many of my readers a simple question: what scares you?

The answers were very surprising. Dozens of people had very standardized fears. One would say spiders and would cringe at the thought of a spider crawling across their skin, while another would be terrified of snakes and things that slither through the night. Many people were afraid of the dark. In spite of my asking in the middle of Michigan, many people were afraid of sharks and wouldn't go into Lake Michigan for fear that there was actually a shark there. Still others were afraid of strange things that go bump in the night. A few people were afraid of vampires and some of ghosts. I want to focus though on one young lady for a moment.

I had a young lady tell me she was afraid of nothing. This surprised me as almost everybody is afraid of something, and many people are afraid of a lot of things. As I talked to her, I told her about some of the stories I had written and said they probably wouldn't scare her because they weren't about very much. As we continued, we suddenly came across spiders in the conversation, and she recoiled. I asked her if she was afraid of spiders, and she said that she just didn't like them. When I pushed only a little it became very clear to both her and I that she had a very deep-seated fear of spiders. As she walked away, she said, "I guess I'm afraid of spiders."

Writers and producers have to find some type of formula that gets under people's skins or at least makes them feel that prickly feeling on their skin when they realize that they are alive. As you read through the short stories that follow, there will be stories that don't bother you at all but the approach to the story is to find something that does make your hair stand up, if only a little. Even if I don't help your hair stand up so that your barber can cut it more easily, perhaps I can entertain you with a story with a twist or an emotional consideration.

In my recent book "Another Slice of Fear," I was impressed with the number of letters I got concerning the story "Monster." The story itself meant a lot to me but it also had an impact on many of the people who read it. At the core of the story was the realization that defining the word "monster" is not always an easy thing to do. When you define "monster," it can apply to just about anything. As I was writing in this book and compiling the stories, I realized that there were deeper places to go. In "The Drifter," I once again look at the definition of a monster and consider who the monster really is. In "Flight Delay," I explore humor with a build that tries to get the reader to see further. In "Francis," I look at something that is unknown, and even though that something is unknown, there is a familiarity to it.

I also return and add another chapter to the original story in "A Slice of Fear," "Edges." The new chapter has convinced me to eventually create a novella just for that ongoing saga. The story can be read alone if you started with this book, but I am all in for you going back and getting the other two.

As with most thrillers, there is an essence of attraction, or another intense emotion involved in creating fear in a story. There has to be something in each story that binds the reader or watcher to the fear they are about to feel. Sometimes it is small and subtle and sometimes it is even as deep as love. It is that concept of attraction that sometimes creates a helpful buffer and allows us to be more at ease in the story. As we are at ease, we are also vulnerable to twists and turns and little things that go bump in the night. That is where the thrill comes in, you know it is around the corner, but you want to feel safe in it. Consider for a moment the innocent summer camp, or the fun Halloween with a young babysitter and a few children.

Because I am who I am, there are several stories that play with new pieces or types of fear. My goal over time is for all of these to come together in a future single volume that will keep people up for a little longer than the 15 stories I'm currently publishing per unit. (16 in "Another Slice of Fear") Ooops, 17 in "Yet Another Slice of Fear." I know, I know, who makes up these rules anyway?

I hope you can take a moment and just enjoy getting lost in a story meant to draw you in, and help you find your beating heart. I hope you have as much fun reading this book as I did writing it.

One last note.

Normally I keep my personal life very separate from everything else. There are numerous reasons for this, but as I do so, I am quite aware that I am also a person. In this particular book, two of the stories were written for a family member, and I hope they have a lot of fun with it too. After all, if you're enjoying your day and want to have a little fun, why not have "Yet Another Slice of Fear" to keep your heart pumping?

Flight Delay

"Hey, I'm going to the bathroom, okay?" my husband asked me in a wry voice, knowing how irritated I would be at him.

"You've got about 15 minutes until our flight leaves," I said; "the plane won't wait for you, and neither will I."

"Are you still mad about the blonde?"

"Blonde, brunette, redhead, I don't really care," I was furious at his attitude. "We are done, and when they land this plane, my first call is going to be a taxi, and the second call will be to a lawyer."

"There wasn't a redhead."

I turned and walked back to the simple gate, waiting for some type of answer as to when we could board this already delayed flight. The cruise had been fantastic, and I truly enjoyed laying in the sun next to the pool while he was off doing who knows what. The problem had come when I realized he was not off doing who knows what but instead, doing who knows who. I was walking down the wrong hallway looking for a stairwell when he backed out of a room in his bathing suit and stupid floral shirt. As he turned and saw me, I saw the naked blonde blowing him a kiss. He slammed the door and followed me until I found the stairs and our room. The words flowed like cheap champagne on New Year's, but there was nothing I could think of except giant tits on a cheap blonde. I was done.

There had been only two days left on the cruise, and I spent them as far away from him as I could. I went to the purser and finally convinced him to give me another room, but somehow Sam had found me. It didn't matter, I didn't open the door, and I didn't look back, and if I could have gotten another flight home earlier, I would have. Instead, here I was stuck in an airport with a dumb ass who cheated on me and had just admitted that it was multiple times.

I have to admit that I knew already. I wasn't an idiot, and I could have guessed quite some time ago that he was having affairs; he never let on and always treated me nicely, so I let it go. Sitting in an airport watching his luggage while he did whatever in the bathroom was insulting enough for me to go crazy. I didn't, though; I sat and waited, and waited, and waited for Mr. Wonderful to walk out of the bathroom.

"Attention passengers on flight 187, we will be delayed another 35 minutes while we switch crews. I apologize for your inconvenience, and Well Spent Airline will happily comp you one premium beverage if you come up and pick up your certificate."

I knew I could use a drink at this point, so I gathered my luggage and Dudley Dimwit's single bag and struggled over to the counter. I was surprised the line wasn't long, but it rapidly grew behind me. I guess no one wanted to be the first to rush up and get their free drink. I showed the somewhat frazzled young lady my ticket, and she handed me a sparkling pass that would get me one premium drink at the bar across from the gate or one premium drink once we boarded the plane. I wasn't waiting, so I dragged the bags to the bar and slapped my sparkling pass of doom on the counter.

"Strong and spicy, please, you pick." I giggled at the bartender, who looked like he got out of diapers four days ago. Was I that old that everyone looked like a child now? Looking up to the bar back mirror, I realized the answer was pretty much yes. I could honestly feel sorry for Stanley Stupid if it wasn't that he didn't dump me first before he dipped his wick in every lamp he could find. I used to be a damn fine-looking woman, the woman in the mirror was old and worn despite the fantastic vacation, well up until Mister Meathead showed me his true colors.

"Ma'am are you okay?" the little bartender asked.

Oh my God, now I was a ma'am. I couldn't help it; I just started crying.

The man, who could be my son or my grandson from the looks

of it, put his hand on my arm. "Don't worry, it's gonna be okay."

I composed myself for about 6 1/2 seconds and then started crying again. Through my sobs, I began whining, "No, I'm not okay. I just looked in the mirror and saw an older woman I didn't know. My husband is a cheating bastard, and I'm not sure how he gets to sleep with 25-year-old blonde bimbettes named Bambi, and I'm going to be a divorced old widow with 15 cats, watching reruns of old Gregory Peck movies within six months. Add to that that my wonderful husband is a lawyer, and I will probably get $3.11 for my troubles, and shipped off to Alaska to be wolf food by the court."

"You're still a lovely young lady, ma'am. It will help if you stop selling yourself short. Yoda said it best, 'Always in motion is the future'."

I wanted to rip his face off or kiss him, and I didn't know which would be better. I probably tasted like an old woman by now, and he would throw up just by kissing me, so instead, I downed my drink, fixed my face the best I could, told him, "Thank you," and walked back to the waiting area dragging my bags and Wee Willy Winkies' across the floor. I made sure to drop his a few times just in case he had something breakable in it that would mess up all of his clothes.

I was nearly haunted for a moment as I continued watching the gate attendant and wondering if we could please get on the plane. Time continued to pass, and every clock tick battered my heart with the force of the evening surf. Once again, the gate attendant took to the microphone and announced with dread that we would be delayed for another 45 minutes. Could this get any worse? The alcohol worked a little, but it did nothing to remove my frustration from James Blonde's secret missions into other women's mysteries and the dark depths of the men's room. I smacked his bag for good measure, knowing that I would probably hurt my hand before anything happened to him or his pack. The cute little bartender brought me another drink, told me it was on the house, and then winked at me. Maybe I wasn't such an old broad after all. I smiled for a moment and thought about teaching him about the birds, the bees, and some other bees when I saw him go into the men's bathroom.

I looked at my watch and realized that Paulie Poopoo had been in the bathroom for over 20 minutes. I was used to him grabbing a book and getting lost inside our home bathroom, but when we were out, there never seemed to be a bathroom he wanted to stay in for more than 30 seconds. His majesty's tender bottom might become infected with the fleas of the common folk if he stayed longer than that. I waited.

A few minutes later, my mysterious bartender with the beautiful blue eyes and crisp haircut came out of the bathroom and went to a utility closet. He pulled out a mop, a bucket, and put a sign in front of the bathroom. He began mopping the floor and then pulled a little ribbon across the door once he had moved the mop bucket inside. The yellow neon ribbon said, "closed for cleaning," and the bartender and mop bucket disappeared from my sight.

I wondered, could that bartender clean up a mess as big as my soon-to-be-ex problem? Would it be easy for this young man to shove my mentally deficient husband down a garbage chute or into a giant garbage bag that could be easily dropped into the Atlantic Ocean to feed the ever-hungry schools of sharks? My mind was running rampant, and I laughed to myself while I closed my eyes for a minute.

A short time later, I heard the counter clerk announce yet another delay. One of the engines was now operating out of range. I wondered how an engine could run out of range. Does that mean it wandered off from the plane? Are there out-of-range engines flying around on their own without airplanes? As I came to my senses from my brief nap, I realized Seriously Stupid Sam was still missing. There was no mop bucket, cone, or tape across the bathroom door, and I had no one around me. All I had was his bag.

I got up and struggled across to the bar again to the cute little bartender who flirted with me when I needed it.

"Yes, ma'am?" he asked in a perfectly polite voice with absolutely perfect diction. His black slacks, white shirt, and black vest made me wonder if he was a Chippendale dancer after hours. I got lost in that thought for about 10 seconds before I felt like I should be put on a child protection list.

"I'm sorry to bother you, but my husband has been in the bathroom for almost an hour. Did you see him in there when you cleaned the bathroom?"

"No, ma'am," he said; "there was no one in there but me. Airport regulations say that I can't have anyone inside when I clean just in case I make someone uncomfortable."

My brain raced in two directions simultaneously. The first was, of course, where was my irritating partner, and why hadn't he come back to the gate. The second was a thought about how I would enjoy this young man making me feel uncomfortable.

"Are you sure there was no one in there?" I asked.

"Sure, ma'am. I double-check every stall, and I cleaned everything for the evening."

I looked outside at the darkness and wondered where all the daylight had gone and how all the light seemed to have been drained from my life over the last several days.

"Is there a security stand somewhere?" I asked.

"Yes, ma'am, it's right over past gate 31. It's not very far."

I looked up at the gate and noticed I was at gate 27. Looking down the brightly lit hall surrounded by the darkness of hundreds of windows, I saw gate 29, then gate 31. Next to gate 31 was a small sign with a badge on it.

"Thank you," I said, looking far too much at this young man's eyes before I wandered down the beckoning hall dragging Phillip Fuckups's bag behind me.

It didn't take long for me to get to the security desk. Two men were looking over a series of papers and checking off boxes while they stared at a computer screen. I was amazed they still used paper. I stood for a moment while the short, stocky black man noticed me. His uniform was pressed, and his shirt buttons and badges shined like a morning sun. I had not seen this perfect a uniform on anyone before, and I was more than a little impressed. He smiled at me, and I felt at ease almost immediately, even though I was irritated, angry, hurt, upset, old, and in serious need of another drink.

"May I help you, ma'am?"

There it was, I was a ma'am again. "Yes, Sir, my husband and I are on flight 187, and he went to the bathroom about an hour and 10 minutes ago and hasn't come back. I asked the gentleman cleaning the bathroom if he had seen him, and he had not. The young man said it was policy to ensure no one was in the bathroom when they cleaned. The problem is, I don't know where my husband is, and eventually, I hope our flight leaves. Do you think you could look around or page him?"

"Yes, ma'am," he scribbled on a piece of paper. "What is his name?"

"Samuel Carter," I replied. "He's 6 foot tall, 190 pounds, blonde hair, blue eyes, 58 years old, and probably flirting with some girl somewhere."

"Yes, ma'am," he smiled and chuckled a little. "I certainly hope not, ma'am. Can you tell me who was cleaning the bathroom?"

"Of course," I said; "it was the young man at the bar."

"The young man at the bar?" he asked.

"Yes, why?" I was curious why he had asked again. The whole thing seemed rather strange to me. The second security guard looked up and looked down towards the bar. The two looked at each other and the short, stocky man talking to me said he would take care of it.

I walked back to the gate and watched as the security guard walked into the bathroom. Minutes passed, and the gate attendant announced that we would begin boarding very soon. I fumbled with the bags and turned around in time to see the bartender again cleaning the bathroom. The line was across the door, and he wandered in with the mop bucket once more. I wondered how the bathroom could have gotten so dirty so quickly as I had seen no one walk into that doorway while I was watching and waiting for my unfaithful idiot of a husband. I turned as the gate attendant stated that it would be just a few more minutes and she would be preboarding. I checked my ticket and ensured I had my passport, and when I turned back around, the bathroom was clean and open. It was fast, and there was no muss or fuss. The bartender was behind the counter again, and I had no security guard, no husband, and no way to know what was happening.

I stood up and looked at the gate attendant as she fumbled with a couple's tickets. They were ranting and raving about something useless, so I drug my bags and one extra hindrance to the security desk, where the second security guard still stood checking his sheet of paper. "Any word?" I asked.

The man looked at me, confused. His security guard outfit was near perfect as well, but he was considerably older and now looked as though he had seen a ghost. He looked down towards the bathroom and seemed unsure. Picking up a radio, he clicked it and asked for Carl.

I was honestly a little taken aback. This was a strange turn of affairs, a bathroom where people disappeared. You usually had to go to a bad movie to see something like that, but today it was happening in the airport I was trying desperately to leave.

"Carl, are you there?" There was a pause and just nothing. "Ma'am, go back to the gate, and I will go take a look."

"Okay," I said gleefully, or at least in a lively manner. I walked back to the gate and watched yet another man walk into the bathroom. I was getting tired of struggling with Sam's bag. I sat and waited and heard the gate attendant announce preboarding. What in the world is preboarding, anyway? How do you board before you board? Behind me, the bartender was cleaning the bathroom yet again. I watched the mop bucket disappear with him and saw the gate attendant struggling with an older woman in a wheelchair. A woman more senior than me, I couldn't believe it. I wasn't sure what to do. We were in first class, and the gate attendant announced that first class was boarding now, and I had to make a choice. I looked back at the bathroom, and the yellow neon ribbon was still across it. I took my bags and Sam's loathsome luggage and struggled down the gangway until I got on the plane. I quickly stowed my luggage and threw Sam's in the overhead. I sat down and stared at the monitor in front of me as it showed a little plane sitting at an airport, waiting to take off.

I stared at the little plane and wondered if I was about to fly off into the wild blue yonder alone. The idea excited me for a moment. I would have a few days to get ahead of it all while he was stuck here. Still, I was a good person, right? What should I do? How should I approach this? Maybe he found another blonde and was flying home with her instead of me? How in the hell did the bathroom get dirty again?

People filed into the airplane one at a time and shoved their bags into overheads. One after another, they passed me—one after another, a series of never-ending people. I looked to the back of the plane and saw tons of seats left to fill and remembered how many people were in that waiting area. I was overcome for a moment. I was probably stupid, but I stood up and walked against the flow of people.

"Ma'am, you need to sit down," the flight attendant said.

"I'm sorry, my husband is still outside. I need to go check and see if he's coming," I said.

"You need to hurry; we will have to close the doors once we

are full," she said.

I ran back up the gate against dozens of people coming down. Why was I running? Why did I even care? I came out at the ticket counter, and that gate attendant asked if there was a problem.

"My husband hasn't come up yet. I just need to find him," I said. "I think he's in the bathroom."

She nodded, and I ran to the bathroom. It didn't take long. It was only a few feet. No one was in the bathroom door, and I looked around the corner and said, "Sam?"

There was no answer. I slid into the hooked entrance to the bathroom and looked at the brilliantly clean floor. This had to be the most spotless bathroom I'd ever been in. I felt dirty being inside a men's bathroom, and as I turned the corner, I saw the row of urinals that sparkled white. In addition to the urinals, six stalls cascaded to the end of the hall. Each one had a stone wall around it and a lovely door. The 6th was more comprehensive and obviously an accessible stall.

I walked to the first door and opened it. Empty. Boy, I wish this person had cleaned my bathroom. I had never seen a toilet seat sparkle like this.

I went to the second door and opened it and once again was greeted with lemon freshness and significantly clean tiles and walls.

The third door was cracked a little, and I opened it, and nothing was there. I was apprehensive, and I didn't know why. Why was I in a men's bathroom when I could have been sitting in first class sipping on margaritas?

I opened the 4th door and fear fell upon me as though I had opened the gates to hell but instead was welcomed with the heavenly scent of fresh cleaner and crisp porcelain.

The 5th door was open, and it too was clean and unique. How in the world could someone keep a bathroom this clean?

I put my hand on the 6th door and pushed it open. I looked in that stall and stared for a moment. I felt a lump rise in my throat, pulled the door closed, and brushed off the handle with my blouse. I did so with each entry until I reached the first and saw the little bartender standing at the door.

"You should catch your plane, ma'am," he said with a gleam in his eye. "I hope you have an amazing flight and a spectacular life. I'll clean up the doors, don't worry about a thing."

I returned to the flight and passed the gate attendant as she waved me through. I reached the door seconds before the flight attendant closed it and found my seat. I sat down and asked for a drink and then a second and stared at the little screen as the plane took off and headed for my home. In the back of my mind, the 6th door was burned like some bizarre etching that I would never be able to get out of my head. When I opened the 6th door, my husband was in a stack of bodies on the floor. He, the security guards, and four others were stacked almost perfectly in clear plastic bags in a neat and clean, tidy stall. I didn't know how, I didn't know why, I didn't even know what to say; I just knew that I didn't have to worry about divorce anymore.

Francis

Jimmy has always been a little odd. He's been my next-door neighbor since we were six, and as we entered high school, we just drifted apart. I went with the more mainstream group and became a cheerleader, just like every all-American girl would want to do, and Jimmy became that kid that sat at the back of the room and gazed out into the sky while the rest of us were lost in this world.

If you think about it, Jimmy probably had it easy. He was so brilliant that he didn't have to study or sit around and do homework. He was funny to the people around him, but he only engaged when they engaged him and spent far more time daydreaming and drawing on his 'filled with graffiti' notebook. From the outside, he was an average person, and although I didn't think of him as a friend anymore, we were friendly. He always spoke highly of me to others.

This afternoon, as I was walking home from school, he joined me. I usually never saw him on my walk from school, as he often stayed at school late, studying in one of the labs or talking to the biology teacher. As we walked together, it was awkward at first. I asked how he was doing, and he said, "Fine." I asked questions about how his parents were, and again he said, "Fine." There appeared to be no rhyme or reason to it, and the more we interacted, the more I wondered why we were walking together at all.

"What are you doing for your science project this year?" I was honestly curious as I hadn't started on mine.

"I've been working on an interface where I can talk to insects." This was obviously of interest to him. "I've spent a significant amount of time developing a pheromone and micromagnetic pulse interpreter that should give me the ability to talk to higher orders of insects."

"That sounds awesome," I wondered about all the ants and being able to tell them to leave the house. "Have you tested it yet?"

"I began testing it last week and was super stoked with success. I was working with a Polistes Dominulus, and I couldn't believe how well things translated. I was able to have her navigate a maze for some honey just by teaching her left and right. It was one of the most awesome things I have ever done."

I could imagine him sitting in his room playing with his wasp, and of course, my mind wandered. I almost giggled to myself but kept it in. "That sounds awesome," I lied. "How do you think you're going to do?"

"I'm not sure it's gonna matter," he looked distraught for a moment and then said, "I already have my next two years planned out, and the science project won't give me much of an advantage. What are you going to do?"

I was on the spot now since I had brought it up. "To be perfectly honest, I don't have anything. My parents don't have any time to help, and I know it's my responsibility, but I think I've over-committed to everything, and never seem to have enough time."

"There's always the stand-by baking soda volcano." I know he was being sweet, but it was almost like a slap in the face. How could he be so bright and me so not clever?

"I think I can come up with something better than that." I was a bit irritated at his smugness. "I was just curious after last year with your rocket engine. Did you ever find it?"

"Well, kinda," he was a little awkward about the whole situation. His rocket engine had gone up so fast that everyone lost sight of it in a second. "It appears that my rocket is in geosynchronous orbit. Every day at 4:00 AM, I am in range of the tracker for about an hour. There's a tiny solar panel on it, so it may run for a few years or more and let me know that it's out there, but as of yesterday, the orbit is exactly the same as when I launched it last year."

"Oh my God." No one had ever told us about his last project.

"Yeah, I say that too," Jimmy pulled out his phone. "This is the picture from this morning as it passed the International Space Station. NASA has called a few times when they pick up the signals."

The picture was very clear, and you could easily see the space station's solar panels. "That's a really clear picture."

"Remember, I launched it with a disassembled Android phone as the brains. I put the cameras from the phone on the front and sides of the rocket. The whole insertion period is on video."

I was irritated that he had become so bright while I had become popular. That's not how it's supposed to work. I was supposed to be the center of attention and the brain.

"If you would like to come to see the project, I would love to show it to you." It seemed that Jimmy was in earnest, and I felt a little bad about my negativity towards him.

"I would like that." I lied again, but in the back of my mind, I thought if I could get something out of Jimmy's intelligence, I wouldn't have to work so hard.

The house was just next door to mine, and we soon walked up his porch. The last time I had been in his house could have been as much as four years ago when I scraped my knee, and his mother bandaged it for me since both my parents worked. The house was a large Victorian kept in near perfect condition by Jimmy's father, a contractor in the area. We used to play in the house when we were young. It had eight large rooms on the first floor and six bedrooms on the second floor. Jimmy's two older siblings had moved out, leaving him the entire house to stretch out.

He took off his shoes at the door, and so did I. We walked upstairs to where his bedroom used to be, and he walked past it to what used to be a playroom. Inside was what could only be described as a mad scientist's lab. The room was filled with everything from plasma globes to numerous computers with flashy screen savers or actual running programs doing something I could not discern. There was a kitchenette and a small couch in the room as well. A worn blanket was on the couch that I recognized from years ago when Jimmy and I played in the house.

"This has certainly changed a lot," I said.

"Yeah, when Mom and Dad saw how interested I was in science and technology, they gave me free rein." Jimmy was walking to a corner where several glass cases covered the wall. "This is what I've been working on."

A computer with a strange screen had numerous wires going to open circuit boards on the side of an aquarium. Inside the aquarium, a hundred or so wasps wandered about as wasps do in the wild. On the screen, there were words that were short. I saw "food" and "water," and "prey," to name a few. The words scrolled by reasonably rapidly, and as Jimmy pressed a few keys on the computer, the wasps seemed to perk up. I looked around Jimmy to see the word he had typed was "honey" and then he pressed a button, and a small dropper extruded a single drop of golden liquid to the center of the aquarium.

The wasps immediately went to the center and competed for the single drop, all except one. That one seemed to be watching Jimmy or me and was not as interested in the antics of the larger group. Jimmy put a small container to the side and slid a small door open, and that one wasp walked into the container. Jimmy then closed the small door and moved the container to another workstation. He put the container on the side, slid open a door, and the wasp buzzed a little, walked into the large area, then turned and looked at us both again.

"This is Francis," Jimmy smiled. "Francis is the one I have worked with the most. Watch this."

Jimmy typed into a computer connected to this particular aquarium. "Hello Francis."

The screen sat for a second, and then the wasp began moving.

17

A small second screen could see a close-up of Francis as the computer typed out, "Hello, Keeper."

"Keeper?" I was slightly surprised that the words seemed to come from a wasp and that they made sense.

"Francis knows she's a prisoner," Jimmy was typing; "I'm not sure if I should release her because she may not return. The lifespan of a wasp is not very long, but they appear to have a significant amount of information they can pass down generation after generation by DNA. Francis is a queen and can live up to a year, but most wasps die within a few weeks. I have only been working with them for about six months, and her children in the other area pick up rudimentary commands from birth. She is far smarter than they are and can command them very easily. She works like a translator when I am talking to them."

I was a little freaked out. Bug boy here was talking to a bunch of wasps and giving them names. "Why Francis?"

"Mainly because she likes to sing. Hang on, let me show you." Jimmy fiddled with a speaker, and it clicked on. He then typed, "Can you sing for Audrey?"

The answer was actually kind of funny, "No."

"Can you sing for me?" Jimmy had a funny look on his face.

Francis began vibrating her wings in different directions, and suddenly I heard the sound from the speakers. It sounded like something out of a lousy opera, but there were noticeable note changes as Francis sang. In the end, it lasted maybe a minute.

"Thank you," Jimmy typed.

"But how can she do that?" I was freaked out about the singing more than anything else. "I mean, she's not a musician. She's a bug."

"There was a study a few years ago in Michigan about the

intelligence of wasps. I think that study didn't go into enough detail. I was playing with cell phones and found there was a certain frequency that a wasp reacted to. I spent six months here starting to translate simple pictures into words and actions that could be interpreted and sent from this console. I rebuilt it for the larger group, and it wasn't until I got a queen, Francis, that I didn't have to start over all the time. Like I said, most wasps only live a few weeks, meaning I had to start over with new ones that I would capture, but Francis has had two advantages. First, she will live much longer; second, she is laying eggs in the nest in the other aquarium, and I no longer have to catch wasps. This makes it easier for me to manage."

"Is Audrey, mate?" the screen flashed. "You are changed."

"What does she mean by that?" I asked.

Jimmy typed, "No," and then looked at me. "She knows who my mom and dad are, and wasps are very good at differentiating people. She knows the difference between objects very well too. If you left the room and returned, she would know you were Audrey. If she didn't see you for days, she would still know you were Audrey. For her, though, she applies wasp logic: females are in charge and mate with males. I have explained to her that it is different for humans. She understands, but I suppose it is a difficult concept for a wasp."

"Audrey is lie," the screen said.

"And what does that mean?" I was feeling a little concerned.

"I'm not sure." Jimmy typed back to the screen; "Audrey is friend." Then he looked over at Francis staring at me.

"No," the screen said; "Audrey is lie."

"What does she mean by lie?" The silly bug was starting to make me nervous.

"She understands a lie, but I've never seen her interpret a

person as a lie. At the start, all she ever asked for was to be free, and when she asked, I would say soon, and eventually, she said I was lying. It is a pretty straightforward concept in the animal kingdom, I suppose. I said something, and I didn't deliver. Since then, she has come to terms with being captive but still doesn't like it."

"Are you going to let her go?" I asked.

"I'm not sure that would be a good idea." Jimmy was a little worked up. He typed "honey" on the screen, and a dropper placed honey in the aquarium as he turned to me. "She's no super wasp, but she understands a lot more than most wasps do. When I removed the need for her to hunt and kill, and took away all of her natural predators, she became like an information sponge. If I'm right and this information is passed downstream genetically, it might not be a good thing to let her loose in the wild. On the other hand, it would control itself relatively quickly because she no longer fears predators and can actually identify many different types of animals as predators."

"You know this is a little overboard for a high school science project," I laughed.

"Yeah, but it got you to talk to me." Jimmy moved closer to me. "I've missed you so much, Audrey, over the years."

I stepped back, not sure what to do. I am sure Jimmy thought that maybe there could be something between us, but I was sure not feeling the same. "I'm not sure what you're thinking, Jimmy, but I was just curious. I better go home."

"I just missed my friend," Jimmy lowered his head. "I had hoped for more but knew you had outgrown me."

"I'm sorry, Jimmy," I said as I went to the door and went downstairs. Jimmy came to the top of the stairs and looked down at me. I turned to see him, and it was apparent he had a tear in his eye.

"Do you think we could ever, like, go out?" Jimmy's eyes were hopeful. "Just as friends?"

"Let me think about it." I wasn't sure why I said that because usually, I wouldn't have even listened; but something today made me feel different.

I let myself out the door and walked next door to my house.

I thought about Jimmy and his fantastic work with the wasps. There was no way my project would be anything near his. I wondered if I would be doing a baking soda volcano again this year.

Our house was nowhere near the size of Jimmy's parents', but it was a lovely house, and I came inside once again to be alone. My parents both worked, and I was often alone for hours at a time. I usually had practice and dance team and would not be home until late; but today allowed me to see Jimmy and to be home alone. I thought about Jimmy again and realized I had grown into a pretty awful person. Sure, everyone wanted to be me, but I'm not sure if I want to be me. Having recently broken up with my boyfriend of six months, I realized that many things I was trying to be weren't meaningful. I set my backpack down and thought about Francis. Maybe Francis could see more than Jimmy was aware.

I left my backpack but grabbed my phone, went back to Jimmy's house, and knocked on the door. It was a few minutes when Jimmy finally came to the door.

"Did you forget something?" It was apparent he was solemn, and I thought I probably just broke his heart somehow.

"Can we go talk to Frances for a minute?" I asked.

"Why would you want to talk to Francis?" Jimmy was a little guarded.

"I think I know why she said I lie." I slid into the door brushing against Jimmy a little but passed him and walked toward the stairs.

"That's a little forward, isn't it?" Jimmy followed me, and

21

soon we were in his overly advanced lab.

Francis was still in her separate area, and numerous words were on the screen. The funny thing was that most of them were sentences. Jimmy tried to block the screen. I pushed him out of the way to see a short conversation about how he liked me and Francis stating that I did not like him.

"This is kind of what I was expecting," I said. "I have to be honest with you. When I came over here, I was looking for an idea. It's been a long time since we've been friends, then somewhere along the way, I found it was a problem to be a friend to you. You just didn't fit in my life anymore. When I sat over at the house, I realized that the wasp probably sees truth and lie a little differently than we do. No, I'm no scientist, but I'm betting I'm right."

"That's a huge assumption." Jimmy was looking at me like a German Shepherd figuring things out. "You're assuming that the wasp can see past all of our truth and lie because her perceptions are much keener."

"Basically, yeah." I sat at the chair in front of Francis. Francis had finished her meal of honey and was paying reasonably close attention to me. It's hard to tell where a wasp's eyes look, but it seemed I was the center of attention, so I typed in, "Audrey likes wasps."

The screen paused, then returned, "Audrey Lie."

I typed into the screen again, "Audrey likes dogs."

The screen paused for a moment, then returned, "Audrey, true."

"That's starting to make sense. I always thought that the reason Frances picked up on things so quickly was simply that she was brilliant. It's more accurate to say that her more complete perceptions of the world allowed her to weed out the things that were unimportant or that were emotional and focus on what was real. Imagine an insect as a perfect lie detector."

"That's exactly what I was thinking." I lowered my head. "When I got back to the house, I thought seriously about how terrible a person I have been. I considered how nice you were and how much I was not being honest with you or with myself." I looked at Jimmy, "I'm not a very good person anymore."

"I think you are," Jimmy smiled; "somewhere inside of you."

The screen moved, "Audrey, true."

"Isn't that cute." I was laughing a little.

"Jimmy, mate," the screen lit up again.

"I don't think I'm ready for something like that." I said as I looked at Jimmy; "but I think I need to spend a little more time away from the people I've been hanging around with."

My cell phone began ringing, and I saw it was Chad. Chad and I dated for six months until I discovered he had been cheating. He was older than me, 19, and unwilling to let me go.

I declined the call, and then I looked over at Jimmy.

"You like me, don't you?" I asked.

"Well, I'm not sure." Jimmy was turning red, and to make matters worse, the screen suddenly said, "Jimmy Lie."

We both began laughing. I looked at Jimmy. "Please forgive me. I will try to be a better friend. I can't believe we both used to chase each other around this house."

My text message ding went off. "I saw you go into the house with that freak."

Chad was texting. I couldn't count the number of times I've blocked him; still, he texted using stupid programs that sent from

23

different numbers every time.

Suddenly, another notification read, "If I can't have you, no one can."

"I had better go," I said to Jimmy. "I'll try to get in touch with you later."

The screen lit up, "Audrey Fear."

"Is that true?" Jimmy asked. "Are you afraid?"

"No, I am not afraid," I was hoping I could get out of sight of the damn wasp.

"Audrey Lie," the screen lit up again.

"What's going on?" Jimmy asked.

There was a crash downstairs, and Jimmy moved towards the door.

"Don't," I said. "It's Chad, and he's crazy." I showed Jimmy the text message, "I know he has guns and knives, and he's just a little too crazy. I think he's coming for me and I'm sorry. Are your parents home?"

"No, I am alone until later. They went out for the day."

"I'm sorry, Jimmy," I said as the door slammed open. Chad was standing there, and he didn't look like someone I had ever dated. He was mussed and furious.

"What are you doing here with this freak?" Chad waved a small gun. It was small, but I knew it was more than enough to hurt either of us.

"We were just talking about a science project," I said.

"I like science. Why don't you show me the science project?" Chad yelled.

Jimmy walked up to Chad and said, "You need to leave. Get out of my house."

The speakers behind me began buzzing, and I heard the now familiar music, only it was much different. Something weird was happening. Chad shoved Jimmy to the ground.

"Trying to steal my girl, you little worm?" Chad growled as he pointed the gun at Jimmy. "Maybe it's time you meet your maker."

The buzzing was getting louder, the speakers hadn't turned up, but the buzzing was incessant.

"What the hell is all this buzzing crap?" Chad yelled.

The screen behind me was scrolling at high speed. It kept saying, "Keeper Hurt," over and over. Jimmy tried to get up, and Chad kicked him in the face, knocking him to the floor again. Chad walked to the more enormous aquariums with the dozens upon dozens of wasps now covering the glass window.

"Now that's a lot of bugs," Chad rubbed his finger across it, and I saw wasps try to sting glass. I glanced at the screen behind me and saw the screen scrolling with multiple messages, then looked to the screen where Chad was standing, and all I saw was one word repeating over and over from seemingly everywhere.

"Chad, you have to leave. I don't want you to get hurt. You have to leave now," I pleaded.

"Ain't nothing in here gonna hurt me except you. You broke my heart."

"You cheated on me over and over, Chad. You don't want me. You just want to control me," I pleaded as the word scrolled over and over. "You need to go now."

"So," Chad exclaimed, "I didn't love them. I only loved you."

It seemed as though it was getting darker in the room. It was then I saw the window. It was slowly darkening, covered in something I could barely see. The buzzing was intense, almost deafening. Francis was making her music, and all I could hear was buzzing. There was something else, too. It was almost like wood was crunching. I didn't know what it was, but it, too, was both subtle yet pounding in my ears.

"No, Chad, you only love you." I started to walk out, trying to put distance between Chad and Jimmy. Feelings jumped through my mind as I realized this was a situation of my making. I was the evil one here. I knew who Chad was when I started dating him. I just lied to myself about him. Audrey lie.

Jimmy was struggling to get up on the floor, and Chad was grasping at my hair as I tried to get free. The gun was between us, and I needed to get away. I bit down on his hand. He smacked me across the face with the gun barrel. I sprawled across the floor and tasted blood. The buzzing continued to pound in my ears, threatening to burst my eardrums. It was everywhere. I saw Jimmy. He was almost at the window. He seemed to know what was going on. He was limping and hurt badly. Chad grabbed me by the throat and pulled me to my feet. I tried to catch my breath, but he had my throat tight. I choked and gasped, trying to breathe. Through the corner of my eye, I saw the window open and darkness close in on Chad and me.

"What the…" Chad exclaimed.

It was as though the specter of death entered the room. A cloud moved across the room with purpose that no human could easily understand. Chad fell backward, pulling me on top of him, and I felt a million legs crawling all over my body, touching me, tickling every piece of my skin with tiny legs moving in unison to get off me and to their carefully assigned victim. I was in shock from the mere thought of what was happening and could not move. Still, it was what was before me that made me hold my breath as I watched hundreds of stingers press themselves into Chad's face, his arms, his eyes, so many that he couldn't even scream through the agony of so much venom at once. I watched from much too close the needle-thin stingers enter and exit Chad's skin, I saw him open his mouth to scream only to be overwhelmed with even more wasps. His body began to convulse before me, and with the horror unfolding so fast, I simply fainted.

I don't know how long I was unconscious, but I opened my eyes and was on the small couch in Jimmy's lab. Nothing was buzzing, and on the room was still. I tried to sit up, but Jimmy held me. "Take your time. The police are on the way."

I was covered in tears. As I sat up, I saw Chad in the corner, gun by his side, covered with a small jacket. The buzzing was gone, and, on the screen, next to Francis, all I saw were the words, "Keeper Safe."

The memory was burned into me of the event. As Francis had played her music, there was only one-word scrolling everywhere on the large aquarium's screen. One single word, "Kill."

Sunset

Amanda walked into her bedroom to see John sitting on his side of the bed in his pajamas, staring out their window at the slowly setting sun.

"How did you get home?" Amanda set down her purse and walked over to look at her husband's face. "Did the doctors let you go home?"

"They said there was nothing they could do for me," John didn't look up but instead stared and brushed his blue satin pajamas until they were straight. "I didn't see the point of staying there if there was nothing they could do for me."

"There might be something," Amanda pleaded for a moment; "come on, let's get in the car, and I'll take you back."

"I just wanted to watch the sunset from home. Our view has always been so beautiful."

"Well, I want to save you." Amanda was flushing as she usually did when she got nervous. "You don't understand. You have to get better."

John looked up at Amanda. "I understand perfectly. I'm sorry you never understood."

"I've always done everything for us." Amanda was adamant. "I never wanted this day to come. I never wanted you to be sick."

John lowered his head for a moment. "No," it was nearly a whisper; "you just wanted to be comfortable."

"I wanted us both to be comfortable." Amanda was standing above John. "I wanted to spend retirement together. Let's get you back to the hospital."

John looked up at Amanda. "They said there was nothing they

could do for me. I tried to call you before I came here, and I think they tried to call you as well, but we didn't get an answer."

"My phone is completely dead. I put it on the charger."

"I'm sure it is dead. It's the most important thing in your life. You spend every waking moment revolving around what is on that phone. You have Tik Tok videos, Facebook posts, LinkedIn, Snapchat, and dozens and dozens of people to text, and I was always right here. You lost the passion for me somewhere in our life, but I still have it for you. Every single day I tried to show you how much I cared about you, and every single day something was more important than us. You found a way every day to avoid affection, to skip by those passionate moments we used to share, and to definitely avoid being physical with me."

"You know that I couldn't." Suddenly there was emotion in Amanda's voice. "It just wasn't the same."

"I know," John lowered his head again. "I know all of your statements and excuses better than you do. I was stupid enough to think you were having an affair for a while. Then I found out you weren't. I was at one of the bars you went to, watching while you had a drink with Zach. I was so surprised that it was just business because I thought someone with your passion had to be with someone else and just fell out of love with me. I blamed myself for a while but then realized it had nothing to do with me. It sounds old-fashioned, but it would have been nice to be together daily. I don't think you ever understood that I love you. I don't think you know what that means. Instead, you had excuses and reasons for avoiding me. It didn't matter what I did or how many times I asked. You set your limits, and I had to live with them. You loved me the best you wanted to, perhaps the best you could."

"It wasn't just me. You said so." Amanda's tears were rolling.

"I lied to you because I love you." John looked out at the sunset in the fiery sky. "I thought that somewhere inside you knew the truth and that someday I would become important. I wish that had been true.

"Watch the sunset with me for a second," John said as the sky became a fantastic series of colors punctuated with puffy willow wisp clouds.

On the charger in the other room, Amanda's phone began to buzz. "Hang on, let me grab that."

Amanda walked into the other room and picked up her phone. A dry voice answered, "Is this Amanda Story?"

"This is Amanda." Amanda walked back into the bedroom and saw the colors of the sunset start to fade.

"Amanda, this is Doctor Phelps. I'm sorry to say that your husband has passed away. There was nothing we could do for him. I'm very sorry."

Amanda looked down at the phone and then at the sunset. She pressed the red button and hung up while dropping the phone on the floor. Amanda fell to her knees and watched the sunset through blurry, tearful eyes in her bedroom, alone, as the sun set on another day.

Captivating Smile

I saw her from across the room. I was sure she didn't notice me. After all, not many people notice me. To my surprise, she caught my eye, and I was mesmerized by that captivating smile that she flashed at me. In disbelief, I ducked my head, embarrassed for looking at such a beautiful woman. When I glanced back up, she was gone. I was disappointed but used to the feeling of not being noticed and being consistently overlooked.

"Hello," a sultry voice said from my right.

I looked up to see that captivating smile and flushed as she looked at me with golden eyes that were both aggressive and cautious, simultaneously.

"Ummm," I stuttered, "Hi."

"I saw you look over at me, and not many people pay attention to me. Well, they do, but then they ignore me because of my height and, of course, my stomach."

It was then I noticed the enlargement of her stomach and the almost absurd protrusion. I had not seen it because of the distance; up close, it was pretty obvious. Her body and frame were lithe and could have belonged to a fashion model, her long raven-black hair was magnificent, but her stomach was pushed out as though she were pregnant, even though it was apparent she was not. "I didn't notice; I just saw your smile."

She smiled again, and I was awash with feelings I couldn't quite describe. I could drown in that smile. I never wanted anything more than to be lost inside that smile. "That is so sweet. My name is Murina."

I stared for a moment at the magnificent woman now talking to me. I was embarrassed and fidgeted, "I am Phillip. Pleased to meet you, Murina. It is a nice name; I have not heard it before."

"It is an old family name," Murina said as she sat next to me. "It was my grandmother's, and her's before her. My family is very old and very proud."

I looked down at my still untouched drink, "I have no family left. Only me."

"What are you drinking?" Murina asked.

"I order a drink, so no one bothers me. I probably won't drink it; I never do. It's just nice to get out occasionally and enjoy being around people. Most people ignore me."

"Why would you say that?" Murina asked. "I didn't ignore you."

"I'm a five-foot-two-inch adult who is just plain. I am an accountant who works from home as much as I do in the office and about the most boring person on the planet."

Murina laughed; the smile was there again. Her perfect white teeth and strong jawline were so alluring. "I am a six-foot-five woman everyone wants to meet until I stand up and realize that my affliction makes me look like I guzzle beer six times a day. It is difficult to explain how people judge you based only on your looks. Of course, some men talked to me but only wanted one thing. I would love to spend time with someone who likes me for me."

I picked up my drink and held it up to her in a toast. "Here's to liking people for being themselves."

Murina smiled and lifted a small drink, and we both laughed, and I actually took a sip.

We told jokes and laughed about everything. Murina was amazingly astute and incredibly funny. She also laughed at my jokes, and it didn't take long for us to giggle like little kids. The night progressed easily, which didn't often happen for me, and it wasn't long enough. As the bar began to close, I felt as though I were lost again. Murina handed me a card and said, "I would like to see you again; if you would like that, call me."

Murina left, and I followed a short time later. I was giddy like a schoolboy and kept thinking back to that captivating smile that made me feel so safe, warm, and loved. Did I just think love? That was ludicrous. Murina was way out of my league, but I considered calling her the next morning. As I walked home, I pulled my jacket tight against my small frame.

Once home, I fed my fish, cleaned up the two dishes in my kitchen, fluffed the pillows on my couch, and went to bed. My dreams were filled with the woman I had just met. I laughed, cried, and repeatedly felt her naked body against mine in my dreams. We slid together naked, covered in oil, and all I could think of was Murina.

Morning came, and I was getting ready for work until I realized it was Saturday. I actually had nothing to do today, so I fed my fish and sat down to watch television. There would surely be something to binge-watch on some channel or streaming service. I went to the kitchen and made myself a bowl of cereal. I looked down at my silly pajamas and wondered what Murina would think of the green dinosaurs and palm trees.

Murina.

She was in my thoughts again. One night, and I had such an attraction to this woman. I thought about it for a moment, then went to my pants and pulled out the card she had given me last night. I dialed the number from my cell phone. It rang once, and then I heard that beautiful voice and imagined her captivating smile calling to me.

"Umm, hello, this is Phillip," I stuttered.

"You will excuse me, Phillip, but I must tell you I have been thinking about you all night and all morning; when can I see you next?"

33

"Well, that's why I was calling. I seem to be off today and was wondering if you wanted to take a walk, go to the park, or see a movie?"

"I would love to go to the park with you; we will have such a good time walking together."

I smiled to myself and suddenly realized I didn't know any parks because I had never walked in any parks. "Which park would you like to go to?"

"There is a little park next to my home," Murina said, "I will text you the address of the park, and you can come here, and we will walk together."

"I love that idea," I was forming the mental image of this beautiful woman who paid attention to a tiny man nearly half her size.

I got the address and walked to the park. It was not far away, and Murina was there waiting for me. She came up and hugged me, and it felt so good. She wore a loose-fitting black dress covering her distended stomach but accentuating her body in other places. She was so beautiful, and that captivating smile caught me immediately again. I was drawn to her eyes that shimmered green and gold in the day's sunlight. I wondered why she was being so nice to me.

Murina reached down, held my hand, and we walked through the park together. We talked about the world and how strange it could be. We talked about her job as an artist. She worked from home, and that was very good for her. We spoke of cruises, travel, and everything else that two people could think of. It was Saturday, and I didn't expect the day to slide by so fast.

Sunset came as we walked back to the entrance of the park. I looked down at my arms in the short sleeve T-shirt I had worn and noticed they were red from sunburn. Murina smiled at me. That captivating smile again. I was mesmerized and had never felt so good in my life. She looked at my arm, lifted it to her lips, and kissed my sunburned skin. I tingled in ways I didn't think I could and was lost in the moment.

"Tasty," she smiled, and we both laughed.

She hugged me and held me tight. I wanted it to never end, and it seemed like it didn't. As she let me loose from her embrace, she lowered her head and kissed me. I had been kissed before, but her lips were intoxicating, and I felt her tongue lightly trace my lips. She pulled away, hugged me again, and said, "Thank you for a great day. I hope we can see each other again soon."

As she walked away, I was entranced by her gait. Her rhythmic walk took her away from me, and I felt that I would die being apart from her. It was an agonizing feeling that I had not felt before, and I found myself wanting to follow, even knowing I should not, could not. She turned, and my heart leaped, then she smiled at me, that captivating smile that I loved already. That captivating smile I wanted to be part of forever.

It didn't take long for her to call after I got home. I was wandering, and for lack of a better word, I felt like I had left something I should have been a part of. You can't imagine knowing how being in someone's embrace makes you feel like you're a part of them and makes you want to be a part of them. I was sitting in my living room, still wearing my shoes, staring at a blank wall, when she called.

"I just missed you and wanted to let you know I was thinking about you," Murina's voice echoed in my ears, and all I wanted to do was hear more. "I can't believe how wonderful you are and what a great day you gave me. All that and you are tasty too."

I laughed at the thought and envisioned that captivating smile and those beautiful lips touching mine. "I miss you already."

"Let's spend some time together tomorrow, too," Murina giggled like a schoolgirl. "I have to go to an art exhibit and would love for you to be my date."

"I would love to." I was already thinking of her lips again. "Where should I meet you?"

"There is a gallery at the corner of 75th and Masterson. Meet me there at noon, and we'll get out when we can."

"I'll be there." I was lost in thought. I kept thinking about her tall body wrapped around mine and how wonderful it would feel to lay close to her and be a part of her forever.

I fell asleep, lost in my dreams. I saw Murina's captivating smile hanging before me as she lowered herself to kiss me. I tried to move and hold her. My dream became frantic; the more I tried to hold her, the less I could move. Finally, I let go in my dream, and I felt her embrace and knew that I would be part of her forever. I felt so good, and she held me and kissed me softly while my mind wandered.

I woke up sticky for the first time since I was a kid. I guess it wasn't that long ago that I was a kid, but the thoughts of Murina were enticing and almost dangerous. I was a midget to her tall frame and felt like she was playing with me. My mind wandered as my insecurities attacked me and assailed my psyche from side to side. How in the world could someone as impressive as Murina have any interest in me? It was 9:00 AM, and I got up and began to get ready. I wanted to be there for Murina. I wanted to give her something that she would remember forever.

By 10:30, I was ready to go and decided to walk. It was 15 blocks to 75th and Masterson, but I was used to walking. A lot of the reason I was so thin was that I walked everywhere. I could eat, and eat, and eat, and never really gain weight, but I had solid muscle mass, and my stamina was near infinite. As I walked, I mused about Murina and how men must be so shallow to cast her aside. Her captivating smile, height, and soft skin made her nearly the perfect woman. Her belly wasn't flat; who cared? It just looked like she was either pregnant or overate at the buffet. Her explanation made sense because she wasn't pregnant, and I hadn't seen her eat at all.

As I got closer to the gallery, my insecurities set in again. I wondered if I should call and cancel. I took my phone out of my pocket to do just that. I didn't want to get hurt again by another beautiful woman who was just playing with me. Why do so many women just play with men and not commit to having them in their lives or with them forever? I put my phone away as I saw the gallery loom near and realized I was now committed when I saw Murina in front of the gallery, scanning until she saw me.

As Murina saw me, she smiled, and that captivating smile called to me. My insecurities were gone. I was lost in the moment, and as we got close, she reached out and hugged me tightly. I felt her arms curl around me, and I felt safe with a woman, probably for the first time in my life. Murina reached down and first kissed my forehead, then lowered her lips to mine, and I felt her tongue retrace my lips. She could have asked me for everything I owned, and I would have given it to her freely. I could not believe the level of emotion I felt for this woman.

Reaching down, Murina grabbed my hand and led me into the upscale gallery, Dante's. The venue was packed with people looking at unique paintings that seemed straight out of the minds of an insane asylum. I looked at one picture and saw a dreadful demon covered in gore and cuts reaching down and ripping the intestines out of a screaming man. Next to that painting was another showing a woman burning at the stake with her flesh melting off and her face forever locked in an agonizing scream. The next painting showed a man being ripped in half by monstrous arms with no face.

One after another, we looked at painting after painting. Each one was gruesome in its own way and each one bordered on the edge of insanity. Some of them were far beyond insane and showed the pits of hell and the demons devouring the souls of men with intense colors and horrible outcomes. Murina held my hand as we walked through, and many people walked toward her congratulating her on her newest work. She introduced them to me casually, and when people asked questions, she explained that I was a good friend she had met recently but hoped I would stay around.

I felt proud to be with this woman who treated me as a person instead of a subhuman because of my height. I felt self-conscious as we met people, but Murina was gracious and constantly made me feel as though I was important to her. As she spoke, she said several times that she expected us to be together. I thought of how that felt and how wonderful it was to have her near me.

As we reached the end of the display, Murina began clutching her stomach and told me that she felt ill. I tried to comfort her, but she said she had to get home. Without warning, she began to convulse and begged me to take her to the bathroom. I did so and helped the best I could, considering she was easily twice my size. Once in the bathroom, she locked the door and left me outside. I heard her inside, and she began to retch uncontrollably. I heard things falling and the clang of items hitting the floor and wondered if she was breaking everything in the room. Over and over, it appeared that her vomiting had no end. I knocked on the door, and there was no answer. I began pounding on the door, and again there was no answer. I felt sick thinking about Murina being in the bathroom alone when I could have helped her. Finally, I heard her whisper at the door, "Can you get me a garbage bag? Just ask Madeline, and she will give you one."

I walked to the front of the room and asked for Madeline. Another tall woman, easily taller than Murina, came to me and asked how she could help me. I told her that I was there with Murina and that she was in the bathroom vomiting and had asked me for a garbage bag. Madeline looked concerned for a moment and scanned the crowd. She looked down at me and told me she would get a bag and meet me at the bathroom. I walked back to the bathroom and lightly tapped at the door. I whispered, "Madeline is bringing a garbage bag for you."

"Thank you," Murina said, "I'm sorry this happened right now. Please go home, and I will call you tomorrow."

"I want to stay here with you and make sure you're okay."

"Madeline will take care of everything, and I will be just fine. Please, I don't want you to see me like this."

I was confused and frustrated, but Madeline arrived and worked her way past me and into the door. She kept the door closed as she slid in. I tried to push through but found that she was much stronger than she looked.

"Please," I said, "I just wanna see that you are okay."

"I will be okay. Please go home. I don't want you to see me like this. I can't let you see me like this."

I walked to the door while watching the entrance to the bathroom. I didn't know what to do as I didn't want to leave, but I didn't want to be a burden. Murina was still in the bathroom, but Madeline came out carrying an entire garbage bag that was tied shut. I thought about going back but didn't. I thought about many things as I walked to a waiting taxi and went home.

As I walked into my humble home, my phone rang, and it was Murina. "I am so sorry," she began, "I didn't want you to have to see me like that. It happens occasionally, and I usually feel horrible for a day or two afterward. I know the timing is bad, but can you wait a few days to see me?"

"What happened?" I was more than curious; I was concerned.

"It is my condition," Murina was tense on the call, "Sometimes my body gets rid of the buildup in my stomach. I feel much better now."

"When can I see you again?"

Murina was silent.

"Are you still there?"

"Yes, I am here." Murina's voice was different. "It is complicated now. I really like you, Phillip. I am a lot. I don't want to hurt you."

"Are you tired of me already?"

"No, you are sweet, but it is not good to be around me right now." Murina's voice was strange. It was different than before.

"I want to see you," I said as I felt my insecurities grow.

"I am sorry," Murina said. "I am not sure that would be good for you."

"Please." I was nearly begging.

"I have to go, Phil; you are adorable." Murina was almost sad, but the line went dead, and I heard the familiar click of my phone resetting.

I sat down in my chair and thought about her captivating smile. Her beauty intoxicated me, and she was interested in me. I was lost, and I began to cry. I knew nothing about this woman, but I was crying over her after a walk in the park and a few hours in an art gallery. I dried my tears and walked to my computer. I knew nothing about this woman.

I looked up Murina in my zip code and got nothing. I didn't know her last name but thought about the art gallery. I went to their site and found a page, "The exhibition of Murina Bodie." I looked up her art and was flooded with results. She had been shown worldwide, and there were pictures of her everywhere. I scanned the pictures; in each, her height and distended stomach were apparent. She was with someone, usually a man of short stature like me, in multiple images.

I scanned through dozens of pictures, and there were dozens of men. None could have been more than an inch or two different from me. I saw her captivating smile in each picture, and a tear welled up in my eyes. Who were these men that she didn't talk about? What happened to all of them? Were they discarded as easily as I was?

I suddenly had more questions than answers and wanted to know. I began looking up each of the men and found little. It was obvious that whoever they were, they were more secretive than me. I felt emotionally exhausted and suddenly tired. I left my computer on, went to bed, and took a nap.

When I woke, I returned to the computer, moved the mouse, and looked at the monitor again. I had a lot of windows open where I had been searching and began to close each tab as I looked at them again, still pining over Murina's captivating smile. What about this woman made me want to be close to her? My life was so much easier only a few days ago, and now I felt borderline obsessed. I texted Murina, and there was no answer. The text was simple, "I miss you." I watched my phone like some stupid teenager expecting the screen to change. There was nothing. I looked back up at the computer and saw the gallery. At the top, there was a workshop event. In it, I saw a call for models. The ad read very clearly.

"Are you a small man with big ideas? Are you interested in modeling? We are looking for men between 25 and 40 years old with thin physiques who will model for a new exhibit. Models must be under 5'4" and be willing to travel extensively."

Below that was a link, and I wondered if this was connected to Murina. I read further that a live casting would be done later this week. Something wasn't making sense, and I was going to find out what it was. I continued to search for Murina and found very little. There was an excellent article in an art review about her work and the fury that it suggested. There were a few articles from churches about how her work was demonic. Most articles praised her progressive approach to painting, and many focused on how her strokes were methodical and near perfect on the canvas. I thought about the venue and how dramatic each picture had been. My mind wandered, and I thought about holding her hand and being close to

41

her. I thought about the kiss and how I was lost in her smile.

I went back to bed and slept through the night. In the morning, I went to work. It was another uneventful day. I didn't talk to anyone as usual and noted on my calendar that I would be working from home the rest of the week. As an accountant, we were free to work from anywhere, and I rarely took advantage of it as much as I should have. I had other plans now. I wanted to know if I was so easily replaced.

When I got home Monday evening, I texted Murina again and found that my account had been blocked. I felt powerless and went to my computer looking for ways to get around my blocked account. I was surprised that numerous apps would allow me to change my number and still send texts. I downloaded one of the apps, which was pretty straightforward. I sent Murina another text and told her I missed her. A moment later, I got a reply asking who it was, and I simply answered, "Phil."

My text was blocked again, but this time the app was more ingenious, and when it found the text was blocked, it simply changed the number. I was trying not to be annoying, but I sent another text and just asked, "Please talk to me?" I was blocked again. I set my phone aside, made dinner, and got ready for bed. I needed some type of resolution. I needed to know why I wasn't good enough.

Tuesday came, and the live casting was to begin at noon. I put together a headshot and a cover letter using my computer and thought it came out pretty good. I dressed conservatively and took a cab to the gallery. Once there, I saw the line outside waiting for the doors to open. There were at least 30 men, all my height. Most were smaller than me. I must have been on the high side. All of the men were dressed nicely. I paid the driver and got in line.

Immediately before the opening time, a limousine pulled up. Five women got out of the car. All of them were incredibly tall. They filed into the building, and I realized the last woman was Murina. I watched with fascination as she walked in. She was tall, beautiful, and smiling that captivating smile towards us all as she waved.

I was now determined, and it was barely five minutes later that the line began filing into the gallery. We were being herded in like cattle through multiple lines, and there was excitement in the feverous conversations going on around me. I kept to myself and was quiet as I was corralled into the door and to a series of five tables. A group of young women dutifully reviewed documentation, headshots, and other information about each person and then sent some forward. At the same time, others were asked to leave and walked out saddened or indignant. People moved away in front of me until it was my turn.

I was eyed, and the young woman before me asked about my modeling experience. I told her I had none but was a quick learner. She reviewed my documentation and asked about what I did, family, and friends. She noted the job would be intense, and I may be gone for extended periods. I explained I had no ties and could go where necessary. I was then moved forward to a second line.

The second line was much smaller, and the men were quiet and patient as they waited. They were shepherded, one by one, into a room at the back. Candidates left, and a new person was taken into the room. Eventually, I was told to take my papers and go into the room.

Five women sat behind desks with a podium in the center. Papers were taken from me, and I was asked to step up onto the podium. I did so and saw Murina was busy writing in a notebook. She looked up and saw me. I could not read the expression on her face. Was she sad? Was she angry? It seemed as though she was unhappy.

One woman asked me to take off my shirt, and I began doing so as Murina gestured to a man to the side. The man walked to her, and she whispered. Shirtless, I stood, and the other four women took notes or checked boxes. Murina spoke up.

"Thank you for your time," she closed her books, and the

security guard came up and ushered me out. I put on my shirt and didn't protest as I walked back into the gallery.

"Miss Murina has asked you to wait here for a moment," he said as he stood like a sentinel next to me.

Murina was beautiful. She was even more stunning than the first time I met her. She was in a tight black dress with a low neckline that showed her curves better than any fashion model. It was then I realized she was thin, very thin.

"Phil," Murina was soft-spoken yet pointed, "Please, this is not for you. Please go, please."

I looked at her and the now near pout. I was mesmerized and enthralled by her beauty. Just a few days ago, I held hands with her. Just a few days ago, she kissed me. "Was any of it real?"

"It was real, Phil, but let me go, at least for now," her eyes were focused on mine. "Please don't press."

I lowered my head and turned on my heel. I walked out of the door.

Once home, I turned on the TV, and the news came up. I saw dozens of police cars outside a building. I realized it was where I was today. The gallery came into focus, and several women were being led out in handcuffs. Dozens of men were still there milling around. It was a parade of short people. I turned up the volume.

"...DNA evidence verified the human remains found belonged to Anthony Fazzelo, son of mob boss James Fazzelo and associate of Clarence Fitch. The remains were found in a garbage bag in the east river, but by a stroke of luck, a ticket stub was found from Dante's. Other DNA found matched a case over three years old for Mario Maguzine. Mario went missing, but DNA was found in his home that previously had no match. Police have arrested four women with suspected ties to the crime based on similar DNA evidence, but according to sources inside the precinct, no exact DNA match has been found. The women, who have admitted they are sisters, have not spoken to the police, but their press agents have released a series of posts documenting their innocence. This will be a case that is popular on social media, as Dante's has a large following on most social media platforms."

There was a knock on my door. I turned off the TV and walked to the door. Murina was there. She looked side to side, then pushed in. She wore a long jacket, and her arms were crossed over her chest. She was hunched down as she walked in, and her makeup was messed with weird patterns on her face.

"I am sorry, Phil," she paced nervously, "I should not have come. I had nowhere to go."

I tried to steady her, "It will be okay. What is going on."

"It won't be okay. My sisters have been arrested, and I have to leave town. I just need a few minutes to get my head together."

"What do you need?" I asked.

"Nothing, everything, my god Phil, I really like you, but you weren't supposed to be you." Murina walked away, seemingly unsteady.

"What do you mean?"

"When I met you, I went to the bar Jimmy Fitch goes to. I thought you were Clarence Fitch. You were so nice and sweet, and I just enjoyed being around you. Then the park and the gallery. It was all so perfect. You, Phil, you are just so nice and perfect."

I was a little confused. "What is wrong with that?"

"Everything, nothing, it is just, well, you are so sweet." Murina slowed down and sat down on the couch. "I need to change. Do you have any scissors?"

"Of course." I went to my knife block and pulled out an

45

unused pair of sheers.

"Can I use your bathroom?" Murina stood.

"Of course." I led her down the hallway to my bathroom. It was clean and substantial for a bathroom.

"This is perfect." Murina reached down and hugged me, then walked in and closed the door.

"Should I call someone?" I asked.

Murina opened the door. "No, just give me a few minutes."

I sat down and waited on my couch. I didn't bother turning on the TV or getting a book. There were butterflies in my stomach. I wondered how I could help Murina. She was my dream come true. I sat for a minute, thinking about her smile and being lost in the feeling that she was everything I ever wanted. I wondered if she wanted me or if I was as insignificant as I felt.

A few minutes passed, I heard the bathroom open, and footsteps approached. Murina walked into my living room. She was completely naked. She looked down at me. "I need you, Phil. I am sorry."

I was looking at a goddess. She was so tall. Her long black hair was now cut short to a bob. It was only to her shoulders, making her height even more apparent. Her skin was without a single blemish; it shone like alabaster and seemed to shimmer ever so slightly as though she were covered in a fine mist of powdery flakes. Her arms and legs were toned to perfection; the muscles were tight, and I could see the power radiating from her. Her breasts were perfect and pouted upwards as though she were a teenager, but her stomach, which had been distended, was now a near-perfect six-pack. I gasped a little at the thought of her needing me.

"Don't be sorry," I said as she sat beside me. I put my arm around her. We began to kiss. Her tongue traced my lips. I felt as though I was in a bit of heaven. I started panting. This was so fast. It was my dream. I pulled back and smiled, and she smiled at me again, that captivating smile. I was lost in it.

She kissed me again, kissed my ear and my neck. She whispered in my ear, "You will always be a part of me. Thank you, Phil." I felt a pinch on my shoulder, then I felt warm and good, it was a dreamy feeling. I felt my clothes come off. I shuddered in anticipation even through my haze. I couldn't move easily but tried to kiss Murina, and she kissed me back. It was so warm, so perfect. I was on the floor, naked, and Murina was standing over me. She smiled at me, and then her jaw seemed to grow or fall; it was as though it separated. I dozed for a moment, lost in her embrace. I felt warm inside and out, and as though I was in a tight hug from Murina. I loved her, and as I opened my eyes for the last time, I saw her beautiful smile, this time from the inside.

Bartender

I'd never seen anything like this. The two customers at my bar were locked in a verbal battle over politics. The politics I had seen before. Most bar fights start with women, politics, sports, and religion. These two men had taken it to a new level, and although occasionally I asked them to close it down, they kept making it more and more personal. I honestly didn't know what to do. As they started screaming, people either got involved on one side or the other or just left. After about an hour of screaming at each other, I went to them and told them, "Either you two keep it down, or I'll call the police on you."

One of the men quickly said, "Yeah, call the police but don't worry, we'll defund them soon. I know my rights better than you do."

The second man started laughing. "Yeah, let's defund the police, and then the only people that will be protecting you are the ones like me willing to stand up for freedom."

"Guys, I don't care." I was pretty livid at this point. "I don't care if you're liberal, I don't care if you're conservative, all I care about is whether people are buying drinks and having a good time. You're making both of those difficult."

The two men nodded but were obviously not very happy about my display of passion towards neutrality. The good part was I went back to tending bar, and nobody was paying attention to them anymore. Every once in a while, one or the other would tap on the bar a little more heavily, trying to make a point. People ignored them, and eventually, so did I.

The bar started slowly waning as we got closer and closer to last call. Eventually, I sent the staff home. It was me, a man sitting in the corner in a blue denim jacket with a Cincinnati Reds baseball cap, and the two men still discussing the right and the left of the political arena.

"Aren't you two done yet?" I said as I cleared their empties and wiped the bar down. "Bar's gonna close shortly. You two need to sober up. How in the hell could you keep talking for that long?"

"This moron wouldn't listen to anything I had to say," the gruff man in the red flannel shirt said. "All he wants to do is give the world a free ride so that people like me can work their butts off and support the losers."

"Yeah, this moron thinks that he's the center of the universe and that anything he makes is for himself and not to be shared with the world," said the second man, who had a fuzzy beard and a series of bracelets on his well-tattooed arms.

Neither man was big nor small, so I wasn't worried about them. Both of them were normal, except that one was extremely liberal, and one was extremely conservative. With the bar almost empty, they began talking louder and louder again until finally, I looked at them and shook my head.

The third man walked up to the bar and stood behind both men. "Can I get a bill?" he asked.

The man in the red flannel looked back at him. "Hey, buddy. You look like a reasonable person. Do you think the world should be free?"

"There is nothing free about the world," the newcomer said to the two of them. "Everything we do has a price, and those not willing to pay the price should be eliminated. It is the law of the jungle and the way the world should be."

The liberal broke in very quickly. "If somebody doesn't have a purpose, they should just be gone? No Social Security or welfare? Should children just be put to death? Are we going to go back to the dark ages?"

The Cincinnati Reds ball cap looked lightly to the side at the more liberal man. "There are obvious exceptions to each rule.

49

Children are the world's future and should be cultivated if they are taught to make a difference, but they should not be given a free ride because if that free ride is taken away, they cannot survive on their own. At the same time, the children and the elderly each give us wisdom and the future. Our responsibility is to ensure that they are comfortable, as it was their responsibility before us."

"But if they can work or make a difference, they should be working or making a difference," the more conservative man said. "We don't need deadbeats running the world."

"That is not for you to decide," the Cincinnati Reds cap said again. "I have heard much of what you had to say this evening, and neither of you is correct about much. One of you wants to eliminate people who disagree with them. The other one of you wants to stop people who disagree with them, and who might disagree with them later. Neither of you made a reasonable argument; instead, you just wasted your time and the time of the people around you. I didn't think it was possible, but the two of you are more of a waste than all of the discussions on social media."

The liberal man started laughing. "Just another conservative. If I were on social media, I would block you."

"But you're not on social media." I was listening to three people talk, and the man in the Cincinnati Reds cap pulled a screwdriver from his pocket, grabbed the back of the liberal's head, and slammed the screwdriver through his eye socket. There was surprisingly little blood. It was somewhat grisly but less than I had seen in movies. The conservative and I sat dumbfounded as the man in the Cincinnati Reds cap held on to the liberal's ponytail, wiped his hands on the man's shirt, then slammed his face into the bar. Again, I was surprised as I saw the screwdriver protrude from the back of his skull, but there was only a tiny drop of blood around the man's hair.

Neither the conservative nor I had moved. We were both wide-eyed and wondering what was going to happen next.

"I don't think we'll be hearing from that side anymore," the man in the Cincinnati Reds cap said. "Can I get my bill, please?"

I reached into my pocket and went through a folder with the remaining tabs. The man had ordered three Cokes for the night. I would have thought that odd if it hadn't been so busy. "Is this you?" I slowly handed him the receipt, my hand shaking. "Just three Cokes?" I asked with a quaver in my voice.

"That's all I had," the man in the Cincinnati Reds caps said. I was finding it hard to focus, I knew I needed to remember this man, but for the life of me, all I could focus on was that Cincinnati Reds cap and the denim jacket he wore. For the life of me, I couldn't tell if he was black or white or somewhere in between.

The conservative spoke up, "I'm not sure I agree with you but thanks for what you did."

At the same time, I said, "That'll be $3.50."

The man in the Cincinnati Reds cap took out a five and a ten and handed them to me. "Keep the change. I know this will be a little bit of a hassle, and I'm sorry, but I can't abide by this type of stupidity. You probably shouldn't allow people to talk about things like this in your bar. It irritates the honest people just trying to relax for a minute."

"Yeah, thank you." I didn't know what to say to that.

The conservative spoke again, "I'm not sure I agree with you but thanks for what you did."

"Oh yeah," the man in the Cincinnati Reds cap said; "You're a blusterous buffoon that couldn't protect yourself if you were inside a tank. You vote for violence and destruction, but you have no idea what violence and destruction are, and I heard you talking about eliminating people. You couldn't possibly know what taking another person's life is like. Nor do you know what it's like to protect an innocent person and still watch them die. The other guy will be the

51

death of the world with his seemingly high morals that our void of morality. He fights for things he doesn't understand, but you will be the weapon he will use to destroy it all. His narrow-minded vision coupled with your narrow-minded need for violence will be the end of us all."

The conservative went to say something, but before he could speak, there was a screwdriver in his eye as he gasped his last breath. The man looked straight at me as he slammed the second man onto the bar, and the screwdriver's tip punched out the back of his skull.

"You might think I'm a little crazy," the man in the Cincinnati Reds cap said; "but I didn't tell either one of them anything they needed to hear. They wouldn't have listened, nor would they have heard. Everything I said was for you. You were the person that listened to them both and did nothing. You were the person that allowed their influence to seep over into your bar. At the end of the day, you will tell this story. Please make sure you get it right so that people will start to realize that no one wants to hear the rantings of the far left or far right. Then maybe it's time to stop. I know you're sitting there trying to process all of this, and probably the biggest thing you'll remember from this night is the Cincinnati Reds cap on my head. They're a good team. You should see them play in person."

The man turned and walked out of the bar, and the bell over the door rang as he left. I was left with two corpses and many questions. When the police arrived, they asked me question after question, and the man was right. I was focused on the Cincinnati Reds cap. I had no idea about anything else. The news crews came, and I told them what the man said to the liberal and the conservative and then to me. I saw it on the news the next day, and on one channel, I heard only the liberal side while the other channel played only the conservative side, and it made me question why I bothered saying anything at all. Then I thought about the man in the Cincinnati Reds hat and knew what he told me was exactly what he expected to get out. I don't know that I'll ever allow politics in my bar again, but I'll be watching for those people in the background who are listening and ready to act.

Deep

I can't seem to feel my legs. They are cold, and as I try to wiggle my toes or move, I feel nothing in return. I am groggy and trying to be awake even though every fiber of my being cries for sleep or just one more moment of precious rest. I'm cold all over, and as I begin to move, I realize I am in the water. Why am I in water?

As I open my eyes, the darkness around me reminds me of the depths of a cave where you can reach out your hand and still see nothing. I look around and still see no light. To my amazement, there is a glow slightly beneath me as my eyes adjust, and I reach down to it, going underwater and realizing it is the light inside my glove compartment. Just a crack was showing as the compartment was closed. Where am I? Why can't I remember?

I reach up, touch my head, and feel the growing bump on my forehead. In front of me, the steering wheel seems normal, but I wonder if there are now patterns on my skull from hitting the steering wheel with force. I move my hair aside and realize that the puffy hair I spent over an hour on is now damp with the water I am in.

It's so dim that I cannot make anything out. I remember quickly that there was a flashlight in the console that my husband insisted I carry. I reach into the console as soggy receipts stick to my hand like hungry leeches and finally find the small flashlight. I have never used it, just like I barely use anything that my husband gives me for "my own safety." Finally, I look at it as I try to figure out how to turn it on. The casing of the flashlight is molded with some pattern around the bottom and around the lens. The flashlight has a button on its base. I press it, and immediately the inside of my car is lit up. My eyes struggle to adjust to the bright light, and I realize the water is just over my legs.

I shine the light on the window, and it looks dark. I move the light and press it against the glass. The beam shines through murky water for at least 30 feet until it is lost in the muck. A moment later, I notice a fish swim by. I'm not sure what type of fish, but it's a pretty good size, and I realize how much trouble I am in now.

I'm starting to panic and trying to remember where I was and what I was doing. It seems like such a blur, and I strain with the answers just outside my reach. Where was I? Where was I driving to? I'm crying now simply because this is so frustrating, and I wonder if my mind is slipping like my grandmother's did not so long ago.

"Get it together, Dana," I say aloud as I listen to the hollow sound of my once inviting vehicle. The water and the windows now make it sound like the inside of some cold, heartless tomb. I laugh for a moment, knowing that if my husband were here, he would be telling me to try to "relax and let's work through it."

A flash of memory. I know where I was. I was at the hospital when my husband had just finished surgery. It was open heart surgery, and he was doing well and told me to go home. Home was nearly an hour away, and something must have happened. That didn't answer the question of where I was. There are lakes within a stone's throw of other lakes in Michigan, and I could be anywhere from in a river to one of 30 different lakes, and not know the difference. My husband would have said something about identifying the fish to determine where I was, but I wouldn't know if that fish would eat me or if I needed to eat it.

It's so cold. The water is always cold, even in the summer. It is summer, though, right?

I find rapidly that the flashlight is waterproof. I know I have to be there. My husband needs me. He is full of bravado and confidence that most people can't understand, but I know he needs me right now. I have to get out of here for myself and for him.

I shine the light in the water and realize my legs are pinned under the steering wheel. They don't appear to be broken, just held tight. I try to remember how to get the steering wheel loose and lean forward. Suddenly, I am reminded I am still in a seat belt. I try to unclick the seat belt, and it finally works its way loose. I get out of the seat belt, lean forward, and find the steering wheel adjustment. The steering wheel lifts easily out of the way, and my legs are free. I try to move them, but they are numb and not working well. I realize I'm wearing a dress. I looked terrific in this dress; it was a white print with flowers and a lower neckline. It's now a piece of cloth floating in the water, keeping me from moving easily. I look around and realize this is the second time a Nissan has saved my life. The first time it saved my daughter and me right as we were T-boned at an intersection. The car flipped over and flipped back, but all of the airbags kept us safe. I shiver for a moment as the cold washes over me, realizing I have to get out soon. There has to be something inside of the car to break the window.

I look inside the console again and start throwing the useless receipts and papers floating through the water into the back seat. There is very little of anything helpful inside of the console. I get onto my knees in the driver's chair and realize that the water has gone up at least an inch, maybe two inches. This means my time is limited. My mind drifts for a minute as I consider my fear of drowning. I have always been afraid of drowning; how it would feel to choke to death, and watch your life pass you by.

I move over into the passenger seat, reach into the water, and open the glove compartment. The papers are soaked, and my extra sunglasses stare at me with cold, mocking eyes. I look into those sunglasses and see myself with my once-perfect makeup somewhat smeared, and my smear-proof mascara sliding slowly down my eyes, making it look like I am crying the tears of death. There is nothing worthwhile in the glove compartment. I slam it shut and lock away the dead eyes of my sunglasses inside their watery tomb.

I think and wonder where else there might be something I could use to break the window. My husband probably had a dozen things in his console and would have said something useless like, "Why don't you just use the frajamathingy to break the window?" I think I would have slapped him if he said that now. His gray backpack that sits in the back seat of the truck has been the brunt of many of my jokes. He has pulled out towels, blankets, a pillow, water, food, and enough tools to take apart a battleship from the small backpack while I laugh at him for being over-prepared and paranoid. I'm sure that backpack had a bazooka in some hidden pocket that could have gotten me out of this mess in a moment.

Think Dana, think.

There has to be something in this car. He always told me that everything I needed was there if I just looked for it. Where is it? What am I missing? The water is up to the vents now, and I only have maybe two feet left. There has to be something here; I know if I only look, I can find it. I slide over the back seat and look into the cargo area. It is full of cases right now, and there is no way I can get to a tire iron or something inside the car without significant work. I have plenty of time, or at least a few minutes, before I face death by one of my greatest fears. I consider gasping on the water again and cough for a moment, involuntarily. I wonder if my husband misses me; and then throw that thought aside. I know he misses me. He wants me to be safe. I shine the flashlight to the side and hold on to the rubberized grip of the housing. It makes me feel confident that I will get out of this knowing that this little item is in my hands. The seat is jammed, and I cannot move it enough to make space to get to the tire iron.

I move back to the front seat. I'm not sure who the engineers were at Nissan that made this new submarine, but I'm very impressed with its design. If adequate propulsion systems were installed, I would drive back up onto shore or down whatever path I needed to be on. My dress is being a pain. I know it is a problem, so I take it off even though I will be cold. I have no idea where my shoes went, but I'm sure they're under the seat or floating around somewhere in the water. Not sure why I thought of that, but I'll set it aside.

I shine the light around and feel the water reach the underside of my bra. Funny, my bra and panties match today. That must mean I wanted somebody to see it. Maybe I just wanted to be buried in matching undergarments.

I have to stop thinking these negative thoughts. I'm missing something. I shine the light around the car's cockpit again, casting odd shapes with the molded front focusing the light. I look at the flashlight and touch the tip of it. This isn't a dollar store flashlight; this is one of *his* flashlights. I look at the molding and realize the words "tactical" are blazoned on the barrel. I can hear my husband telling me, "Strategic is being prepared for everything. Tactical is to be used in the moment."

A tear wells up in my eyes. I had it in my hand the whole time. I'm mad at myself, but I am going to be okay. I breathe deeply. Is the air getting stale? It's not going to matter. I take the front of the flashlight, hold my breath and slam it into the window. The design of the flashlight is such that maximum force is put on minimal space, and the glass shatters easily. I thought it would be more challenging. There are jagged edges I smash as I begin to realize the clock is ticking. There is no more air. It all rushed its way to the surface, and I have to clear a whole lot of this window, or it will reduce me to sushi as I swim out. I used the flashlight, and the bright beam has not dimmed at all. I slam into the pieces of glass, and they fall away easily under the onslaught of solid steel. The window is open. I push my way out, careful to avoid the glass. I see bubbles going up and remember watching a movie about following the bubbles.

The bubbles are faster than I am, but I'm a good swimmer and keep kicking with my cold legs. My lungs strain and are begging for me to take a breath. I know that if I do, everything is over. I push harder and wonder how deep the lakes are. It can't be that far. If it is, I won't survive. I have to survive. I'm kicking and pushing, and the light flashes wildly as I hold it in my hand. There is no light, only darkness. I feel like I'm lost in the depths of a horror story swimming in a darkness that will never end. I can't hold out. I've got to take a breath even though I know it will mean my death. No, I have to hold on for one more moment. I remember a movie my husband and I watched; the medic kept saying, "just one more," as he saved person after person. Now I fight each second, holding myself from taking a breath: just one more foot, one more stroke, one more. My muscles are tensing, and I know all they want is oxygen; all I want is to be able to breathe—just one more moment.

My head breaks the water's surface, and I gasp and blubber. I cough over and over and look around. I cough again and can see the bridge and the gap where my car went over the bridge. Two vehicles are stopped that I can see, and people are pointing at me. I swim to the shore of the park where I have seen so many people fishing and enjoying the river on the edge of the lake. I'm on my knees coughing. The flashlight in my hand lights a path towards me. I roll onto my back and feel the mud squeeze into me as the warm summer air blows across my cold body. The memories flood in of the moments before the crash. I was crossing the bridge between the two parks. Two deer rushed at me, hitting the front of the car as I slammed into the guardrail. I remembered the car tipping and falling into the water, and the impact as my head hit the steering wheel.

I look up to the night sky, and my flashlight shines a path into that sky. I have done this. I saved myself. No one was necessary but me. As people ran up to me, I stand in my bra and panties unashamed, knowing that I overcame something that many could not, and I did it by myself.

For the Asking

Tara felt the noose tighten around her neck. It would not be long now. The crowd had gathered as the day progressed, and she had been led out to the makeshift gallows pyre just a few minutes ago.

"Isn't this a little overkill?" she asked the black-masked executioner.

"One can never be too careful with a witch," the gruff man-monster replied. He towered over her as he checked the noose and the pullies above her. "We will hoist ya from here, and yer neck will break. You will dangle as I light the fire beneath you. It will purge yer soul and remove the foul demon inside."

"She deserves no explanation," the black-robed priest shouted. "She has been tried and convicted of witchcraft and heresy to the holy church of the state. All she deserves is death."

The monster bowed to the smaller man, and his tongue was silenced. He was no more gruff nor measured, just quiet as he did his work. His eyes under the executioner's mask scanned the small priest but did not challenge him. The priest went forward to Tara, "Are you ready to confess? You may be given forgiveness by the Almighty if you confess yourself as a witch. It does not matter now. You will die either way, but perhaps your soul can be spared."

"I am no witch," Tara spat. "I am just a wench that refused your advances. Better you kill me lest you suffer the pain of my truths being told."

"No one can hear you, child," the priest said as he looked around. "Perhaps this is a more pleasing outcome for you than my manhood."

"I have heard tell there is no manhood under those robes, just the instrument of a child," Tara grinned.

The priest slapped the woman, and the crowd cheered. He smiled only a little. "Out ye demon!" he yelled and hit her again. The crowd screamed in applause, and he hit her again. "Release her spawn!" The crowd was as excited as the priest beat her over and over, and with each blow, they yelled in approval.

"You see," he said; "they know you are a spawn of evil."

"It's too bad they don't know you are the evil one," Tara said as blood dripped from her split lip and battered eye.

"Now you look the part, witch." The priest smiled with the nasty smirk of a nocturnal predator. "You should have taken another path."

Tara spit blood, spraying it on the wood stack next to her. "I suppose death is better than laying with you."

The executioner snickered. "Buffoon, silence, or you will join her!" the priest yelled.

The monstrous hulk of a man again went on about his work, stoking the kindling and setting the rope to be sprung when he pulled. It was pretty ingenious. Instead of a fall, a trebuchet pulled the man or woman up from the ground with massive force, snapping their neck, or at the least, knocking them cold. It did not go up far. When the lever was pulled, the fire was lit as well. The executioner pulled a long edge broadsword out and began running a stone down its length.

"A sword fight? At least that would be fair."

"No milady," the hulk stated as the stone made a slick sound up and down the blade. "Once the fire is out, I will separate your head from your body and bury it in a separate grave."

"You take your job seriously," Tara said.

"Oaf," the priest slapped the executioner; "I told you to be silent."

61

The executioner stepped to the side and sheathed the intimidating sword. On the hilt, Tara noted the cross. "He is a man of god, yet you have him do your bidding? You are an evil priest."

"Perhaps," the priest replied, "but I will not die today."

"Hear me, people," the priest yelled; "the demon will not confess, but we all know she has been possessed. She is a witch by my own sight. She attempted to seduce me and plotted to steal your children. See her blood; the righteous will not feel. She is surely a spawn of hell." He coughed once, twice, thrice, and continued. A small cloud of dust was in his face.

The executioner reached to him as he coughed and held him for a moment.

"The demon has changed bodies; it attacks the priest and will soon have us all!" the executioner yelled. With swift motions, he cut Tara free and pulled the noose from her head. "Quiet, if you want to live," he whispered. The noose was replaced on the priest's head.

"Pray for the priest, for surely his soul is safe," the executioner said. The crowd was stunned but was starting to chant.

"Burn him! Burn him!" they cried.

Tara leaned to the side, holding her battered body up. The executioner pulled the lever as the wide-eyed priest gasped for breath and reached for the noose, his hands were not bound, but he was too slow. The counterweights dropped and spun, and he was pulled five feet in the air in a split second, and the crowd cheered as they heard the familiar crack. The executioner lit the pyre under the ropes, and it began to burn, soon it was too hot to stand near. He walked Tara to a safe distance.

"You must watch and profess the demon is gone," he said.

"I will do so," Tara replied as the fire blazed and the body jerked fitfully while the water began to burn out of it. They watched to the end, and as the fire started to die, the body fell, and the woven rope finally gave way to the flames.

The crowd was still watching as the executioner pulled his sword and severed the head from the body in one stroke. "It is done!" he yelled, lifting the skull with a gloved hand for all to see.

The crowd cheered and began to mill around as though they were unsure what to do. Several people walked to Tara, and she said she was finally free. Each blessed her, eyed her with some semblance of respect, nodded, and then moved forward. Within an hour, there were only a few men left cleaning the area for the next burning.

Tara looked at her savior as he took off his hood. He was not a handsome man nor ugly; he was a massive bulk of sinew and scars from forgotten battles or untold beatings.

"Are you okay?" he asked.

"Sure, I am well," she said and walked beside him. "What is your name?"

"I am John," he said; "son of John from a line of executioners."

"How many have you killed?" Tara asked.

"I have lost count, milady," John replied. "It was with no pleasure I killed anyone; it was my job. Not so long ago, I realized it was a ruse, and the priest was evil. I have been waiting for such a time."

"I thank you for that, but how did you make him cough?" Tara asked.

John pulled a small bag from his pocket. "Ground cinnamon. It clouds the lungs."

"That it does," Tara replied.

"May I walk you to your home?" John asked.

"I have no home," Tara said. "It was burnt down when the priest took me."

"Then you may stay at my home tonight, and I will sleep in the barn."

They walked a short time to a small cottage with a barn and shack near it. There were no neighbors, and the day was nearing twilight. A few chickens roamed the area, and miniature pigs and goats were in a small pen to the side of the barn. "This is home," John said.

He opened the door. The inside was a dirt-covered floor with a small rock fireplace. There was a bed on one side, made of stuffed straw, skins, and blankets from around the hut. It was surprisingly clean. John took off his sword and hung his cloak. His massive arms were bare. He grabbed a blanket and set it by the door. He went to the fireplace, and the coals were still hot; hanging over the fireplace was a pot that he opened.

"It is not the best, but it is a nice stew," John told her. "You are welcome to it."

"I am not hungry now," Tara said. "I will eat later."

John nodded in understanding, took a small, hammered bowl and filled it, then sat on an oversized chair and ate. As he finished, Tara sat on the floor next to his chair.

"Thank you for saving me," she said.

"I am sorry I could save only you," John replied.

Tara moved behind the chair and began rubbing John's neck. At first, he resisted, but soon he was relaxing, and she kneaded his large shoulders and neck muscles as he closed his eyes. "Does that feel good?" she asked.

"Yes, ma'am," John replied as he sat still feeling her hands massage him.

"John," Tara said.

"Yes?" John asked.

"Do you believe in witches?"

"No," John said. "I have yet to see one I believe in."

"You have now," Tara said as she rubbed, and he slowly began to shrink in her hands. He did not hear nor care; it felt so good. His massive body withered and bent, and as John faded from this life, he just thought about how good it felt to save someone. Behind him, Tara smiled, her wounds healed and her body was made whole. She pushed the lifeless husk to the floor, took the bowl, and made herself some stew. The food tasted as good as the life she had just taken, and she smiled at the thought of another day.

Hunger

The hunger had come again. It was worse this time and ached far worse than any she had felt before. It was likely brought on by the lack of suitable meals. In this modern world, no one was pure, and they polluted their bodies and minds with impurities that she had never imagined possible. She wondered if her hunger would ever be satiated again. It had been so long, so very long.

She walked down the busy street in downtown Lansing. People wander past her, oblivious. Her loose pants and hoodie covered her well and hid her from prying eyes and the glaring daylight. To most, she was invisible. As she walked, she breathed in and nearly choked. Most men and women around her reeked of grease and oil, and their minds were full of hate and avarice. How had this race survived? If only it were the days of old, and she could hunt the mighty Buffalo or majestic Moose. Now, they were so hard to find and burdened with human interference. In the days of old, there was food as far as the eye could see. No one missed the minimal amounts they had to eat. Like the predators who used to rule the land, the wolf, and the bear, and the eagle, they took only what they needed. Now it was all at risk; now there were few places to hunt and even fewer that were pure. The once massive forests filled with purity now felt the complex carbon and the animals scattered in fear far too easily, making the hunts difficult. To find the pure now took time.

She caught the scent of purity as she turned the corner next to Jimmy John's fast-food store. Turning, she followed until she held the smell and saw that it was a young woman of perhaps 20. She kept her distance and cautiously blended with dozens of people walking in every direction. Her situational awareness allowed her to navigate without watching them as she fixed her gaze on her prize. The downtown thinned, and soon they were in a small residential area. It wasn't long before the woman entered a modest house that seemed all alone.

Cautious, she backed off and found a boarded-up house only a few feet away. She knelt, folded in upon herself to become the smallest she could be, and waited. The next morning the young woman left the house again, and she followed her. The young woman walked with cautious abandonment to the courthouse. Hours later, the young woman left and returned to the home. The boarded-up house with its ill-maintained lawn and bushes offered protection and the perfect location to watch her new prize.

The next day came, and once again, the young woman walked to the courthouse, stayed for a few hours then returned to the house. There was a purity about her that she had not sensed in a long time. Her lean body was in good shape, and it was apparent from her scent that she ate well and ate correctly. This was going to be glorious.

She followed the woman for days. At last, her patience was to pay off. She could feed in peace as no one came or left but her from the modest house. She planned patiently, followed back from the courthouse the next day, and waited. Sunset came covering the horizon with the blood-red colors she desired. Her patience was about to be rewarded, and though her hunger cascaded across every fiber of her being, she could ignore it for a few more hours.

Darkness was upon her, and she knew it was time. She worked her way across the street to the modest home and waited for the lights to turn off. She crept to the side and then the back of the house, and found the door locked. She had seen the inside of these locks; the tumbler system would be good against humans. She grasped the door handle and turned it with enough force to snap the pins and open the door with relative quiet. Peering into the house, she saw nothing. She slipped into the door and closed it behind her.

Moments later, she worked her way through the room and was stunned at the sparseness of the area. Where was the furniture? Where were the material comforts that humans so enjoyed? Her caution increased as she looked around the room. Something was wrong. She had hunted humans for hundreds of years, since they became the easier prey.

She saw a pin light that glowed red to her right and realized she had made a mistake. She started to turn, and the lights all came on at once. Not the glowing lights of homes but brazen lights that burned. Spears from the side of the room flew into her body, and she screamed in pain. Chains pulled them tight, and she could not move. Trapped, she looked around and saw the woman she had hunted. There was something familiar about her now.

"Remember me?" the human asked. "You took my mother in front of me and left me as too young to bother with. How does that feel now?"

She looked up at the woman and remembered as the machete took her head. Her last thoughts were simply that there would be no more hunger.

The Drifter

Why can't people understand?

I have tried for a long time to keep my distance from people and instead, pay close attention to myself and the inner peace that seems to be the smallest part of my very being. Many see this inner peace that I seek so sincerely as who I am, but they often find that that is not who I am, and that is when I have to move on.

As I walk down the gravel of another forgotten sideroad, I consider the past several days and all of the actions and interactions that has led me to another long walk to another forgotten town. The brisk wind blows across my face, but I barely feel it. My hands hold my jacket, not for comfort but for the shame of the past few days.

I arrived in Ansel only a few weeks ago. It was a beautiful little town with white picket fences in the downtown; one of the downtowns where modern yuppies rush to and chatter about the overpriced boutiques and the excessive cuteness of the restaurants. I was wearing what I'm wearing now and walked into the town, hoping for silence and peace. Jobs were easy, and I found a job cleaning in a few minutes in a small warehouse right off the main street.

The warehouse owner was in a bad way as the post-COVID landscape had made workers tough to get, and workers with good ethics even more challenging. I told him I could start immediately, and he gave me an extra day to find a place to stay. I filled out paperwork with him using a valid ID and the Social Security number that would allow me to work indefinitely. I was now Derek Griffin.

I had enough money to last for a while. It made it easy to find a small over-the-garage apartment less than a block away from my new job. I didn't usually carry a bag. The furnished apartment was perfect. It even had towels and one roll of toilet paper. This was something people took for granted until COVID happened.

I signed a month-to-month lease. Mrs. Abigail, a little old lady of unknown age and a sharp mind, had several questions but seemed to like me and was hoping for a year's lease. I told her I often had to move on for work but would pay her one month ahead, which seemed to end her nervousness.

There was a drug store in the downtown area and a small second-hand store where I purchased some clothes and got some everyday sundries, including soap to wash the dust of my latest long walk away from my body. It was harder to clean away the memories. Much harder to hide the scars.

The warehouse job was good work. It didn't take long for me to be completely immersed in cleaning, stacking, and loading. My size made it easy for me to carry almost everything, but I knew how to use the forklift and pallet jacks as necessary. My new boss was Mr. Johnson. He was ex-military and, for an ex-Marine, was very calm. I worked extra on the first several days as he was behind and only had two other warehouse workers that were young, inexperienced, and full of themselves. I gave them distance, ate alone, then went home to my new place and stayed awake thinking of the past.

After my first week, I met Caroline. She was the daughter of Mr. Johnson and did some of the books for him. I guessed she was probably 25 but had no real clue and didn't want to get involved. She had other ideas. Each day she would try to talk to me, and I would nod and do my work. As the sweat-soaked my long sleeve shirt and my hands glistened, she would come up and comment about how I needed to slow down and not strain myself. I would nod politely and continue my work, oblivious to the suggestion. I did not need to slow down. All I needed was to find my peace.

In the second week, Caroline stood in front of me with her palm out to my chest and said, "Did I do something to make you dislike me?"

I was a little taken aback. It was infrequent that people noticed me until that time when I had to leave. It was even rarer that someone paid attention to what was happening with me or even cared if I existed. I found my voice and said, "No, ma'am. I'm just trying to be a good worker."

"Well, you're probably the most exceptional worker my father has ever found, or so he says, but all you ever do is work. You stop and eat for a few minutes and keep working. I don't think I've ever seen you take a break, and I don't think I've ever seen you talk to anyone. You look like you need a friend."

"I don't have many friends," I lied. I actually had no friends. Once upon a time, I had a friend, and it did not end well in that story. "I just want to get my work done."

"I don't have many friends either," Caroline was looking at the wall. "The world seems to look down on a single mom who's only twenty-four."

"I don't judge." I was trying to make conversation, but since I rarely made conversation, I wasn't very good at it. I was good at other things I didn't want to be good at.

"You just try to get your work done," Caroline was still looking at the wall and not at me. "It would be nice if you could talk to me for a few minutes because the other workers and everybody else just stare at me or act like I'm an awful person. You don't have to, but it would be nice to have someone to talk to."

I considered for a moment. This was a bad idea, and I had been here before. There were 1,000 reasons I should not talk to this woman and only one reason I should.

"I will take my lunch at 12:30, if you would like to talk." I picked up the vast crates and walked away, leaving Caroline staring at the wall.

I tried to set things aside and find my peace, but I knew Caroline would again be why I would leave. It seemed there was a Caroline, Johnny, or Mary Ellen in every town. Someone who needed something that they thought I could give. I had faced this before and not walked away. Now here I was again. Perhaps this time would be different.

12:30 came, and I sat down on a crate. Caroline joined me with a small lunch box, and we ate relatively quietly for the first few minutes.

"I suppose you have some questions." Caroline was staring out at the open sky through the warehouse doors.

"No, I have no questions." I looked at the sky as well, trying to find some peace in this now repetitive conversation.

"Well, I'll answer the ones that you won't ask. I dated a man in high school that got me pregnant. I have a daughter named Anna. She is the light of my life and makes my father smile all the time. With my mother gone, it is just him, and me, and Anna. Anna's father lives in the area, and I had to convince my dad not to kill him. You know how Marines are, always ready to solve the situation."

Of course, I knew how Marines were. I had learned a long time ago that Marines were tenacious and to give them distance if possible. I had no desire to tell Caroline this, so I just listened.

"I'm a small-town girl and don't want to be in a big town. I would be happy with just me, my dad, and Anna. I'm not dating, and I'm not looking to date; don't worry, I'm not trying to date you. I don't have any friends because Anna's father has pretty much poisoned that well. I'm just me."

"It is good to be you." I kept staring out at the sky and saw the pickup truck pull up.

Caroline saw the pickup too. She stood up and put her lunch away. She walked to the warehouse door as a tall, well-built blonde man approached her. I couldn't initially hear what they were saying and honestly didn't care. I suppose I could have listened, and it would have been easier. Instead, there were suddenly finger points at me and the man pushing past her towards me. It only took a few moments for him to be in front of the crate I was sitting on, asking questions about who I was and what I thought I was doing with Caroline.

I had faced his kind before. I put away my lunch, picked up my lunch box, stood up, and walked away.

"Don't you walk away from me," the man said as he walked back in front of me. "I want some answers right now."

"I don't want trouble, and it would be best for you to walk away." I turned to walk away and felt his arm grab my shoulder and try to spin me around. I stopped, but he could not move me. I turned and looked at him, and he realized somewhere in his mind that he was well overmatched. He was probably 6' 5", but I was taller. He was probably 240 pounds, but I was heavier.

There was a look on his face I had seen too many times. He pushed his finger into my chest and said, "If you don't want trouble, stay away from my girl."

Caroline was indignant. "I am not your girl. Except for Anna, you are the biggest mistake I ever made."

Behind her, Caroline's father walked up, "I 100% agree with that. You do know that you are trespassing right now."

"I'm leaving, old man," the younger man said. "Remember to stay away from my girl. You're not so big that I can't take care of you."

Inside I was saddened. It was likely I would soon lose my small apartment where I felt comfortable, my extra set of clothes, my new toothbrush, and a place that I found peaceful. Why were people always so quick to distrust? Why did people want to test me to my extreme? Why did the people who thought they were monsters not realize there were real monsters in the world?

Caroline looked at me. "Are you okay?"

73

"I am fine." I looked back at the sky and watched the pickup truck leave. "I try to avoid conflict."

"That was Sam." Caroline was obviously angry. "Sam is Anna's father, but there is nothing between us. I wish he would go away, but he never does. I'm sorry that he is such a pain in the ass, and I'm sorry if he bothered you or made you feel bad."

"I know his type." I stared at the blue sky and noticed a cloud that looked a little bit like an elephant slide past the open warehouse door. "I'm not concerned."

Mr. Johnson shook my hand and said, "Thank you for not running away. That boy has run off good help before. People get afraid of him, and they just leave, or something else happens. If he bothers you, let me know. I'll get the sheriff on him."

"He won't bother me." The elephant had moved on, and now there was an earthworm-shaped cloud sliding across the sky. I looked down at Caroline and her father. "I'm not afraid."

My voice rang with such conviction, I'm not sure they knew how to take it. They looked at me with an uncomfortable silence that closed in around us.

"Well, that's good. Just remember what I said," Mr. Johnson told me, breaking the moment as he walked back up to his office.

"Sorry about our lunch," Caroline said. "I really wanted to know more about you."

"There's not much to say." I looked down at Caroline away from the clouds and my peace. "I am just me."

I went back to work. The two younger guys started following me around. As I stacked crates and unloaded trucks, they began to help more where usually they were nowhere to be found. Normally, the trucks would take most of the day to unload and stack, but with the two extra workers, it went quick, and I began sweeping out the warehouse. The two boys quietly joined. Not a word was said, but when I looked up, they would nod at me with some type of respect.

"Thanks for standing up to Sam," one of the boys said; "this place is hard to work at with him showing up all the time."

I nodded but said nothing and kept working. The last truck of the day came in, and we unloaded it rapidly. It took no time to stack and reload, and the warehouse was in near-perfect condition. It was Friday, and Mr. Johnson handed each of us envelopes. As the two younger men left, Mr. Johnson looked at me. "You sure have made a difference with them. I put a little extra in your envelope just for that."

"Thank you," I said. I gathered my lunch box and walked the short distance to my tiny apartment.

The weekend was uneventful. I made it uneventful by staying in. I helped Mrs. Abigail on Sunday for a few hours with her garage and cleaned it up. Mrs. Abigail told me about her husband, her life, and her children. Her husband died last year. Her children were long since gone, living in California, and she never heard from them. She asked me no questions and just allowed me to listen. I listened and was amazed at how few breaths this woman took as she explained her life history to me.

Monday morning came, and I was at work bright and early again. Sam was waiting in his pickup truck, and as I walked to the closed doors, he got out of his truck and walked up to me. Out of the corner of my eye, I saw two other men walking toward me from different angles. "Not even two weeks," I thought to myself. I hadn't done anything and would have to move on again.

"I wanted to do a little follow-up to our discussion." Sam was looking at me dead in the eyes, thinking that I was unaware of all that was happening around me. Sometimes I thought humanity was stupid as they ignored their senses. Behind me, a man was carrying a baseball bat. I saw it as clearly as if I was looking at it, a wooden

75

Louisville Slugger. The other man brought a split 2" x 4". Sam was looking at me dead in the eye.

I looked down at him and saw all the fear in his eyes that he was trying to hide. I whispered to him, "You don't want to do this. I am the monster you fear at night. You will lose."

He paused for a moment. He was unnerved but then suddenly shook himself back into reality, thinking what he saw was what was real. Humanity again.

The baseball bat came across the back of my head and shattered. I'm sure the man that swung it was feeling his hands in new ways as his hands and fingers were not built of the same thing I was. He backed off, holding a shattered piece of a bat. The second man had swung the 2" x 4" across my back, and it too split but did not shatter. I never stopped looking at Sam, but Sam looked at the two men, and his eyes widened.

"It would be good to leave me alone." I started to move forward, and Sam put out his arm.

"You stay away from Caroline." He put his palm on my chest.

I looked down, calmly reached up, and took his hand from my chest. As I moved it away from my body, I put more and more pressure on his arm. Sam began to sweat, and his eyes pleaded until I let go and said again, "It would be good to leave me alone."

I walked into the employee entrance of the warehouse and realized how stupid I was. Perhaps humanity was not as stupid as I was. I could have just walked away and done nothing. I could have stepped away from the men and avoided showing them even a portion of what I was capable of. Instead, I brought attention to myself.

Caroline walked up to me, oblivious of everything that had just happened.

"Hey, big guy," she said. "I brought you a donut."

She handed me a small bag, and I opened it to see a long john and a napkin. "Thank you."

"There are about 20 minutes before anybody else gets here. Why don't we sit down and talk for a few?"

This was a bad idea. I knew this was a bad idea, yet I sat down with her and started eating the long john.

"It was pretty awesome, you standing up for me." Caroline was smiling at me. Why weren't people afraid of me? I was easily twice her size; by that alone, she should have given me a wide berth. Instead, people always thought I was good and calm, and that person they could trust. Caroline turned around momentarily and motioned, and a small blonde girl wandered up. "This is Anna. Anna, this is my friend Derek. Derek works for Grandpa."

I smiled and looked down at the child. I knew what to do and how to try to make people comfortable, but kids were more intuitive than adults. Anna looked at me as though I had escaped her nightmare last night. I put out my massive hand and said, "Nice to meet you, Anna."

The tiny girl took my hand and shook it. Her eyes were always on mine.

"Mama, can I go color?" Anna asked in a voice that was so sweet it would cause normal humans diabetes.

"You go ahead," Caroline leaned over to me. "I have to take her to school this morning and just wanted you to meet her."

"I should tell you that Sam met me at the door. He and two other gentlemen attempted to scare me away."

"Are you okay?" Caroline sounded concerned. I wasn't used to people being concerned about me. I stopped for a moment and thought about it.

"I'm fine," I finally noted; "they couldn't hurt me, and I think they left a little wiser to that."

"Don't be so sure," Caroline said. "Sam is about the stupidest person I know."

I laughed inside. It was the same story again. Someone always wanted to ignore the signs everywhere I went. Everywhere I went, someone wanted to take on the bigger person just to show they could do it. If only I could work without my shirt, and they could see, they might feel differently. Even if I rolled up my sleeves, they might start to understand.

Caroline stood, and I stood as well and put out my hand. Caroline deftly slid my hand aside, moved in, and hugged me. I felt her warmth even through my long sleeve shirt and T-shirt. She held me, and for just a moment, I awkwardly put my arm around her and patted her softly on the back.

Anna walked up as Caroline stepped away from me. "Mama are we going to school?"

Caroline was flushed, and I felt terrible that I had that effect for a moment. It would not be suitable for either of us to spend more time together. I knew I would have to leave anyway, but the hug felt nice.

"Yes, honey, let's clean up so we can get in the car and leave Mr. Derek alone so he can work."

I watched the two of them walk away as I had watched so many in the past. I had to let go of the past, but it seemed it continuously repeated itself. In every town, there was someone nice who only wanted to be friendly; in every town, there was someone ignorant of the world who wanted to be evil. I thought about how long it had been since I had a hug and how good it felt. I set that aside opened the warehouse doors and began to work.

Fifteen minutes later, I was interrupted while stacking a

pallet. Mr. Johnson walked up and grabbed a box next to me and helped me stack a new shipment.

"I saw Caroline was down here with you," he picked up another box; "and I saw those boys outside this morning. It looked like they hit you pretty hard, but it didn't bother you, did it?"

All I needed was one of the good people against me. "No sir. It didn't bother me."

"I've seen a lot of shit in my life, and I've never seen someone take a baseball bat to the back of the head and shatter it. I'm guessing you've got a titanium plate back there, but I really don't want to know. I just need to ensure you don't hurt my girl." He looked down for a moment. "I think I've hurt her enough for both of us by not killing that sorry little pissant."

"If you killed him, he would win. It sucks how the bad guys win if the good guys do what they need to do to make it right."

"You got that right," Mr. Johnson looked out the open warehouse doors; "if I hurt him, I go to jail, and she loses her father. If I kill him, she loses me forever, or he kills me, and she has to put up with him forever. I've been playing a losing hand for too long, and I can tell you that it's obvious that you can protect her better than I can."

"No sir, I can't." I hung my head for a moment, not knowing how to say it. "I will do all I can, but eventually, I will have to move on. I've traveled the whole world moving on because people can't understand what it's like to be me. My," I paused. "My father set me on a challenging journey. I traveled the Arctic Circle; I have been spurned by many and applauded by more. Always I have to move on in the end."

"That's about the most cryptic shit I've ever heard," Mr. Johnson picked up another box almost as big as the one I was stacking. "I would say you're a mercenary, but there's something more to all this, and I'm not going to ask again. You're doing a great job, and those boys working with you respect you and are working more than they ever have here. As long as you're good to my Caroline, you are welcome here; and I'm sorry I didn't come out and stand next to you this morning."

"I'm not a mercenary." I placed the giant box on a new palette. "I'm just me."

"Well, you keep being you," Mr. Johnson said as he wiped his hands and brushed off his pants. "I appreciate you letting me help you."

I looked at him and smiled. I often wondered what my smile looked like, but he smiled back, turned, and walked to his office.

I didn't see Caroline until the end of the day. She was back with Anna and came into the warehouse on her way home. She walked over to me and handed me a small bag, "I got you some food."

"You didn't have to do that." I could smell the food and knew it would taste good.

"If you haven't figured it out yet, I don't need anybody telling me what I can or can't do. If I wanna get you food, I will get you food," Anna looked up as her mom talked to me. "Now you eat that and have a good night. I have some work to do, and Anna will keep me company."

I thanked Caroline, took the bag, got my lunch box, and began the slow walk home only a few blocks away.

When I reached my tiny apartment, Mrs. Abigail was standing in the driveway, wearing a lovely pink moo moo with curlers in her hair. "Are you having a good day, Mr. Griffin?"

"Yes, ma'am." I started to walk up the stairs to my little apartment.

"Do you smell smoke, Mr. Griffin?" Mrs. Abigail turned and

looked towards the area I had just left.

I looked up and saw the trailing smoke go into the air. It has always amazed me how smoke and fire were almost as alive as I was. I heard the sirens in the distance and left my pack and dinner on the stairs rushing back the way I had come.

As I got closer, I could hear the flames, and turning the corner, I saw the warehouse I had just left engulfed in flames. My walk became a run as I made it to the front. Mr. Johnson was lying on the ground, face bloodied, covered in soot, trying to sit up.

"They took Anna," he looked at me with the pleading eyes of a father. "Caroline is still in there. The fire is too hot, and I couldn't get to her."

I saw the flames rising in the warehouse, and it reminded me of so many years ago when I was the target and people tried to set me on fire. I survived and had respected fire ever since. Some people thought I was afraid, but I was not. I knew fire was a primal force that could barely be stopped. I knew what that was like.

I grabbed a hose from outside the warehouse, sprayed myself with water, and then rushed inside as firefighters ran to try to stop me.

The inside of the warehouse was a scene from hell. Flames attacked cardboard and wood, and the heat would have instantly caused an ordinary man to collapse. I looked at the office and saw the door was open. At the bottom of the stairs, Caroline was there. Her body was crumpled on the ground, and I ran and picked her up. She felt limp in my arms. I did not even want to consider the possibility that she was gone. The door was still open, and I ran to it. I curled her as small as possible, so my body shielded her from most of the heat. I grabbed her hair with my arm when it started to spark and realized my shirt was also on fire. I ran faster, and as I entered the air in front of the warehouse, I felt the hose spray down on me from Mr. Johnson.

Paramedics rushed to Caroline, but they all looked at me as well. I stood quietly for a moment until I realized that what was once a shirt was now ashes, and the water spray had revealed the terrible scars all over my body. My wrists bound together by suture now grown together as one. My neck, arms, shoulders, and legs all bore the scars of my creation. I saw one of the people watching gasp as another simply mouthed the letters, "WTF."

Mr. Johnson looked at me as Caroline coughed. "Are you okay?"

"I'm fine." I looked around and saw the truck, then I saw Sam holding Anna in the back of his truck.

I began walking towards them, and Sam saw me. Anna was screaming. Sam's two friends jumped into the back of the pickup as Sam pushed Anna into the front seat and started the truck. I started running towards them, but the truck sprayed gravel as they drove away. I was frustrated until a large F350 pulled up next to me. Mr. Johnson was sitting inside. "Get in."

I got in the truck, and before the door was closed, the giant engine roared to life after Sam and Anna.

"I'm not gonna ask what happened to you." Mr. Johnson was purely focused on the road ahead but spoke as he drove; "I just need to save my granddaughter. Can you help me?"

"Yes sir," I said as he took a corner in a full slide.

"They're heading out to the quarry. The boy is an idiot, and I'm worried about what he may do. Caroline told him to stay away and that she was getting a protective order to keep him away from Anna. He said something idiotic and started beating up Caroline. I knocked him down, and if it weren't for those two idiots he has with him, I would have ended the situation. Instead, he set my place on fire and left Caroline to die. He would have killed me too if all the people hadn't come up."

"I know his kind. They are cowards, and we will get Anna back." I watched the road slide past. Soon we were on the tail of Sam's pick-up.

Sam took a sharp curve on a gravel road, and suddenly we were parallel to a deep quarry. Without warning, he slammed on the brakes, and the two men in the back struggled to hold on and not be thrown from the vehicle. Sam jumped out of the front and closed the door trapping Anna inside. He was carrying a tire iron, and the two men jumped out next to him.

As Mr. Johnson slowed, I got out of the truck and jumped to the ground while the F350 rolled to a stop. I landed with a solid thump and was steady. I walked to Sam and his friends with careful determination. For the first time in a long time, I felt I had a reason for being in the situation I was about to be in.

"You seem to have a wardrobe problem." Sam slapped the tire iron on his hand as he walked toward me.

"Look at his skin," one of his friends said; "he looks like he's been ripped to pieces and put back together again."

"That sounds like a good idea." Sam slapped the tire iron against his hand and winced a little when it struck.

The three men widened out around me. I saw Mr. Johnson over to the side, and he pulled out baseball bat out from behind his seat and started walking over as well. This changed things a little for Sam but not for me. I looked over at Mr. Johnson, then glanced at the cab of their truck, and he understood. Anna was the priority.

"We're going to try this again, and this time it's not going to go as good for you." Sam moved forward and swung at me. I grabbed the tire iron as it swung and held it tight. It vibrated in my hand from the impact, and I know that Sam felt it far worse than I ever could. I pulled the tire iron away from him and threw it into the quarry. I heard a splash.

"All I wanted was to finally be left alone, and there is always someone like you," my eyes narrowed on Sam. "I'm going to ask you nicely to leave me alone. If all of you leave town, this will go easier."

"Sure, we'll do that." Sam was wearing a nasty smirk even though it was apparent that his hand still hurt as he held it. "So, we can avoid the murder charge from killing your ass."

"Just remember," I looked at all three of them; "I gave you a chance."

The two men swung at me from different sides. I let them hit me. Sam swung immediately after, and I wondered if he broke his hand. One of the men ripped the rest of my shirt off, exposing the numerous scars from where limbs had been attached, nerves stretched, and a circulatory system built from scratch. To an outsider, I was nothing but a patchwork man, but I was a miracle born of a man's dream and the living power of the storm. I saw Mr. Johnson get Anna into his truck, and I swung sideways, knocking both men 20 feet into the air. They crashed onto the ground and rolled in pain.

Sam was indignant even in the face of impossible odds against him. He pulled the pistol from his pocket and aimed it at me. I smashed it in my hand, and the pistol exploded as my fingers crushed the cartridges to the point where bullets went off. Unfortunately, Sam's hand was there too. The bloody fingers he pulled away were dark with powder burns as blood ran down his arm.

"You just couldn't leave me alone, could you?" My voice was rising, and I felt pure seething anger. I liked Caroline, Anna, and Mr. Johnson. I liked Mrs. Abigail. I liked my small apartment. I was furious, and there was a tear in my eye as I dropped Sam to the ground crying like a child. "Let's set the record straight on what you're up against."

I walked the 20 feet to his truck and knelt. I slammed my fingers through the side of the door and around the truck's frame right at the edge. I screamed. It echoed in the quarry and through the woods surrounding the quarry. It was a primal scream born out of the storm that gave me life. I stood, and the truck tilted up as I pulled that side off the ground. The truck was now at a 40-degree angle with the tires nearest me dangling off the ground, but I wasn't done. I pulled the truck back towards me in one motion and pushed up. The snap was like lifting a piece of paper, and the truck was now above my head, held by the frame in my hand. My fury knew no bounds as I looked over at Sam and his friends, watching me in disbelief.

"Do we have a problem?" I said in a voice louder than one hundred thunderclaps. I let the truck slide towards me just a little, then pushed it. Muscles never meant to see life again flexed with the power they should never have had as the truck went airborne and landed somewhere in the middle of the quarry. There was a crash, then a splash as the truck sank to the bottom of the water.

I brushed my hands off and walked to Sam. The two men who had backed him up were now huddled together, looking at me in disbelief and terror. I reached down, and Sam cringed as I lifted him by his shirt and felt the threads strain. "Should you join your truck?"

Sam lowered his head. "No." he looked at his hand. "I'll leave town."

"Only to come back later for me? Or for Caroline or Anna?"

"I might be less than perfect, but I'm not that stupid." Sam was sullen and obviously in pain.

"Gonna tell the world and have them come for me?"

"Who would believe me?" Sam was crying. "I'm such an idiot."

I dropped Sam and walked over to Mr. Johnson's truck. He too was looking at me in disbelief. Anna was snuggled into his arms, having seen nothing.

"Should I walk home?"

"No," he said. "Get in. I think I owe you a lot."

The drive back to town was quiet. Anna held my hand. The warehouse was damaged horribly, but the insurance adjuster was already there. Caroline was at the hospital, and I asked Mr. Johnson to drop me off at my apartment.

"Am I going to see you tomorrow?" Mr. Johnson asked.

"It might be better if I move on." I put my hands in my pockets, "I'm not sure if I should stay. Once people learn a little about me, they don't want me around."

"I thought you just wanted to be left alone?" Anna was now asleep on the front seat.

"I just want peace." I lowered my eyes for a moment.

"I can't always promise peace, but I can promise a good paycheck. It looks like we have a lot to rebuild. See you in the morning?"

I looked up at the sky. It was the first time someone had seen even a little of what I was, and they still wanted me around.

"Yes sir." I felt the breeze flow against my skin and knew I needed to change clothes. "I'll be there early so we can get started."

"I'll tell Caroline and let you know how she is in the morning." Mr. Johnson drove away. I walked to my little apartment, hoping that tomorrow would finally be a peaceful day.

I changed my clothes back into the ones I was wearing when I arrived in this little town. I went downstairs and began to walk. I was at the edge of the town and off on a side road, looking at the beauty of the area. I've seen hundreds if not thousands of these side roads. I looked down the road, wondering where it would lead. I turned around, and somewhere in the distance was the city I just left. Caroline and Anna were there.

Perhaps it is time to stand for something. Instead of walking away this time, I've decided it's time to make a stand. Home is only a few minutes away, and I'm sure Mrs. Abigail would miss me or at least my rent. Besides, I have work to do in the morning.

Skittering

It was just another walk down the driveway. Well, I have to back up for a second; the driveway is almost half a mile long and covered with trees, ferns, and everything else from side to side. Walking down the driveway is a nice smooth bit of exercise, and I do it every day to get mail. Today as I walked down the driveway, I was assailed by the skittering sounds of little feet. I usually don't hear anything but the brush of the wind through the leaves and the slow creaking of trees that strain against the afternoon gusts. I was late today, and the sun is slowly setting in the western sky as I wander down my drive. The warm breeze is inviting, and I close my eyes and let the gentle wind caress my cheeks. Because of the way the road winds, I soon cannot see the house or the road, and it seems as though I am alone in the middle of nowhere as I open my eyes.

I hear rustling in the leaves to my side under the thick ferns. I usually can't hear these rustlings, but for some reason, today, it is more prevalent. Typically, the wildlife stays far away, but for some reason, today, it is close. As I look around, I notice the ferns moving, jerking slightly where whatever animal beneath has hit the stalk, making the fern jump and sway. I wonder what type of party the plethora of animals are having underneath the canopy of thick foliage. Is there something exciting there? Is there something exciting somewhere else?

As I walk further down the driveway, I think about the possibility that maybe I am something exciting. My mind wanders, and I wonder how many squirrels, chipmunks, or weasels it would take to knock down a full-grown man. Perhaps there's something more significant under the ferns. Perhaps there's something down there that is excited or even appetized by the thought of a full-grown man or woman.

I start to quicken my walk, laugh at myself, and slow down again. The thoughts rolling through my head are the stuff of silly people who believe in the Easter Bunny and Bigfoot. I look down at my thick jeans and well-worn cowboy boots and laugh at the prospect of tiny teeth trying to get through the fabric. What a series of thoughts.

As I wind another bend of the driveway, it seems like even more ferns are moving, and I wonder how many animals it takes to move the dozens of ferns bouncing around as if buffeted by a swift wind. Could it be 10? Could it be 20? Could it be 100? My mind is in a frenzy for no reason, and my logic continues to shut down the foolish thoughts that bounce into my head, only to have two more replaced in line, trying to make my brain a little more cautious. I wonder if Hercules felt this way as he was trying to cut off the heads of the Hydra. As each head was removed, two more grew in its place, and if he had not realized there was a mystical head and buried it under a rock, he would have been fighting forever until, eventually, the Hydra overcame him.

Of course, that put me back on the path of chipmunks and squirrels. For every chipmunk that I kill, two more appear? How many chipmunks does it take to get to the Tootsie Roll center of a Tootsie pop? I laugh to myself as my mind plays tricks on me while the chittering underneath the ferns grows louder. I know there's nothing there except a few small animals, but my head feels like it's pounding. A swarm of killer field mice could easily attack me at any moment. Their beady little eyes look into mine as they all dive on top of me as though I were some titanic piece of cheese. After all, the cheese stands alone.

The humor bouncing in and out of my head helps keep my sanity as the chittering, movement, and almost constant clatter resonates through the trees. There seems to be an echo from all the sounds, and I'm unsure how so many foreign critters got underneath the ferns without me being able to see them. I lean down and try to see under the ferns and see nothing but the thick stalks of hundreds upon hundreds of small plants. I laugh to myself for a second and wonder if this is how insanity starts. Can a mind become insane just by obsessing over something that doesn't necessarily exist but might? Is the entire process of sanity simply ignoring the things that might be and only focusing on what can be proven?

As I round the next bend, I realize I am walking a little faster than I usually do, and I slow down as the main road comes into view. I feel, finally, a little relaxed even though twilight has embraced the horizon, and soon, I will be walking back to the house in late twilight or the dark. I check the mailbox, which is empty except for a few scraps of paper. Why are there only a few scraps? Did the chipmunks eat my carrier? Did the field mice lunch on my letters? I wish something would eat my bills, but I'd still have to pay them. Maybe I could gather all these chittering animals and send them to my bank to eat all my bank records. That would be amazing, suddenly, to have no records of anything.

I look back down the driveway, and it is no longer peaceful but instead, a series of moving items are calling to me desperately, all of them wanting me; and me, wondering what I should do to survive. I know it is irrational, but I began walking faster and faster, heading towards my house. I know it's not far, but it seemed so far away, and the lights at the house haven't come on yet. I don't have a flashlight with me; what an idiot. I always have a flashlight with me in the dark because it gets really dark in the country. I look up to the twilight sky and see the first stars starting to push their way into view. How many steps does it take to get home? Is it not far now? Will someone please turn off that annoying racket? Why can't anyone hear me?

I realize that no one is going to hear me. There is no one to hear me except the thousands upon thousands of psychotically rabid animals hiding under the ferns waiting to take me to the other side. I know that they are there now, and they are coming for me. I can't believe that after all I have been through, that it will be tiny field mice that find their revenge upon me. I didn't mean to kill her. She was pushing too much. She was always making noise and never listened to me. Why couldn't she have listened to me? Why did she have to push me? When I pushed her back, she fell against the table, and I watched as her head split open and blood ran across the floor.

I called the police but where are they? They should be here soon, but even after checking the mail, the police aren't here. The ferns are buzzing incessantly like a never-ending freight train slamming the sounds in my head. I'm walking faster and faster back to the house, but it seems like the driveway will never end. The darkness is there, and I know that at any moment, I will be covered with bats, and mice, and squirrels, and shrew, and skunk, and possum, and it will be my time. I feel my heart pounding and wonder why everything is so loud that I cannot even think.

I turn the last bend, and I can see the house. I'm gasping for air as I am running toward the open lawn. The giant spotlights at the house come on, and I hear sirens in the distance. They are muffled by the sound of whatever is under the ferns. As I reach the edge of the clearing, I turn and see the thousands of eyes staring at me, passing judgment. They began to move out towards me with mechanical precision and maniacal purpose. Thousands of eyes all start to run towards me as I feel my heart pound and grab my chest. I fall to the ground in painful agony. As my eyes begin to dim, I see the ambulance and police cars pull up the driveway I just traversed. My last view of this world is the thousands of eyes under the ferns at the edge, watching me die.

Surgery

Darla was apprehensive.

The job was supposed to be easy. The surgeon, the neurosurgeon, and her GP all said there would be no problem. It was routine surgery, and the worst case would be that she might not feel much better than she does now. The best case was that all of her pain would be gone.

The surgery included accessing her spine straight through her neck and fusing two vertebrae from the front. There shouldn't be any issue with this as this type of surgery was very methodical and successful across many cases. Everyone involved continued to tell her that it was 99.9% risk-free and that although her recovery would be three to four weeks, they felt confident that she would feel better almost immediately.

Darla didn't care. The pain over the last six months had gotten progressively worse, and anything would be an improvement. Darla looked forward to the anesthesia and the excellent sleep she would get over the next several hours. Her anesthesiologist came into the room and explained that she would feel groggy and then sleep heavily. There would be no side effects. The anesthesiologist went on to explain that she would be well taken care of afterward and that he would check in later.

The nurses came in and ensured that she was in her ill-fitting gown with openings in both the front and back to allow more access to her neck area. The actual procedure would be done at about the center of the esophagus, and she would have a neat scar in the future. There was a final check of all vital signs and a lot of movement. One of the nurses ensured her IV was well set and injected a small syringe into the IV line.

"This is just going to help you relax. You might get a little loopy, but it'll be okay. Is your family here with you?"

"My brother is out in the waiting room," Darla said; "he's probably playing video games right now, but I'm sure he'll come back when I'm done. Typical brother, you know. Lived with him for 16 years and then moved out to get away from him. Now I can't seem to get rid of him."

The nurse checked the chart. "I see here he is allowed to get your status, so I will go out when the surgery is over and let him know, and then the doctor will talk to him shortly after that."

Darla was starting to feel very sleepy. Her eyes were heavy. She felt very relaxed. "I feel pretty good."

"That means the drugs are working, and that's a good thing." The nurse was moving cords around. "We're going to head down now."

The next few minutes felt like a race car drive as nurses moved the bed backward and forward until they were in a large surgical amphitheater. Darla looked up and saw the shapes of people in an upper area and remembered she had signed the consent for this to be a learning surgery. Not many people did the surgery with the new 3D print. The advantage was more mobility after surgery, but the disadvantage was that it was a little more invasive as they rebuilt the vertebra.

A group of nurses gathered around Darla and moved her to the surgical platform. Darla barely noticed and felt really good by this time. A man in a mask appeared behind her and looked into her eyes.

"How are you feeling?"

"I feel most excellent."

The anesthesiologist laughed. "Okay, I'm gonna give you something right now, and I want you to count backward from 10."

"Just 10?" Darla laughed, "I'm a really good counter, and I think you'll need more."

"Go ahead and count backward for me," the anesthesiologist said.

"10…"

Where was I? I remember being prepped for surgery but couldn't remember what happened afterward. I try to look around and realize I can't move. My head is frozen in place, and there is no way I can move it. A light above me flickers, and I try to open my eyes. I'm so tired, and my body feels funny right now. Slowly, I open my eyes and realize I'm inside some type of room. There are windows above me, and it is cold and sterile all around. My eyes begin to focus, and I see the lights hanging at curious angles above me. I'm not sure what's going on, and I feel as though I'm a little detached. I try to move my hands, and I'm stopped as I do so. As the feeling comes back to my arms, I realize I am strapped down and cannot move. I try to focus on what I can, see. That's when I notice that the windows above me are spattered with holes. As my eyes focus further, I see blood on those windows.

What happened?

I have no idea, and as I try to swallow, I realize there is a tube down my throat. I start to panic, and my breathing becomes irregular in seconds. I try to strain, and I can feel my neck tighten and my head held solidly from the sides. I remember from reading on the Internet, about how the head was immobilized, and the body was immobilized so that the patient couldn't move during this surgery. I'm trying to slow my breathing, but I'm overcome with fear as I struggle to understand what is happening.

My eyes swivel side to side as fast as they can, and I see nothing but the shattered windows above me, the spotlight focused on me now dim and cracked, and something on the light above me. Is that blood?

I saw this video game when my brother was playing it, but now I was in the center of it. I was trapped on an operating table, strapped down, unable to move with no one in the room but me. I think this is when the zombies come in and rip my brains out. I'm inspecting every inch of the windows above me and realize a stain is in the bottom corner. At first, I don't recognize it, but fairly quickly, I realize it is a bloody handprint dragging down the window and disappearing. I'm sure somebody is lying on the floor where I can longer see it.

I remember coming into the room and the preparation and the anesthesiologist asking me to count backward from 10. How far did I count? I'm not sure I think I only counted to 10. I tried to scan with my eyes for a clock. I can't see one. My breathing is ragged, and I wish I could get this tube out of my throat. I want to gag but can't even do that. Panic is setting in. I'm straining. Darkness seems to close in on me. I feel my hands tingling.

I open my eyes. I must have passed out. I have to get in control if I'm going to get out of this. I don't know if five minutes have passed or five hours. Where are the doctors?

I breathe as well as I can with the machine down my throat. I'm trying desperately to stay calm, but it's difficult. My first order of business is to figure out my mobility. I move my legs, and they, too, are strapped down. No. A sheet over me keeps me from moving, but I cannot move my legs without knowing about the rest of me. My throat feels a little funny.

I try to move each arm and get some leeway but only move perhaps four inches. I realize the connecting points are actually at my wrist. Moving several times, I realize the bands are not tight. This was not to keep me captive but from thrashing or moving. I try to slide my wrist, and the straps move with me. I try to move them again and feel the strap move down just a little. I try to move again, and the strap is almost to my thumb. I move again, and this time the strap slides up my arm a little. A tear forms in my eyes as I realize I have gone backward. I control my breathing; I don't need to pass out again.

I continue trying to move my arms and finally feel the strap with my thumb. There is a small loop, and I work that loop until my thumb is on the other side of the open hole. I twist my hand side to side and slowly work that strap down toward my fingers. I'm almost there. My fingers push the strap, and my left arm is free.

I move my left arm over to my right and feel pain in my throat and head. I never realized that you also shift much of your body when you move your arm. Given the surgery and my immobilization, I have a problem with doing that. Realizing that there's something wrong, I take my time and lift my right arm while slowly moving my left arm across my body, walking it with my fingertips. I find the other strap and quickly remove it. I am once again rewarded with pain in my head and throat from moving too quickly. I stop and leave my hands together for a moment gaining my composure.

I realized that in the situation that I am in, if I reach up like I usually would, it could be harmful. My shoulders would shift significantly, causing my throat and my head to strain. That could hurt a lot. I try to glance around the room, and there is nothing. I feel around beside the bed, and my right hand becomes wet and sticky. I tap my fingers together, and they stick lightly. It is then that I start to recognize the smell. I smell blood. I wonder if my hand is covered now in blood and try to wipe it off on the sheet. My movement causes pain again. I stop and control my breathing.

I've been waiting too long, and I am not sure if time is on my side. I reach up slowly to my neck and hit steel. I follow the steel across to my neck and realize, to my horror, that both sides of me are being held by small steel bars. As I follow those bars, I touch an open incision in my neck. I can feel my heart racing and hear the monitors beeping, letting the nonexistent doctors know that my heart is racing. How am I to know if the surgery is finished or if my spine is partially taken apart right now? I can't call for help with a tube down my throat, and I can't move, knowing that I could rip my own throat out or worse.

I feel the panic again and realize I am trapped here, alone in the flickering lights. My head is held tight, and my neck is wide open, being held by steel arms so that surgery could be done. My mind is on fire trying to come up with a solution, and there doesn't seem to be one. I want to scream and cuss, and I realize that my breathing is getting out of control again and I'm feeling tingly as I did before. I hear *pops* in the distance. Is that gunfire? What is going on? My eyes begin to go dark again. I try to hold on.

How long was I out this time?

I'm sure this isn't good for me. I realize my neck is wide open, and that is probably not the best way for my neck to be. I wonder if it's packed with gauze or if it's still bleeding. I have to do something, or I will just die here or end up with a permanent hole in my neck as it dries out like some crusty piece of bread. It's time for me to do something. I slowly reach up and feel the ends of the clamps holding my neck open. They do not appear to be pinching skin but instead appear to be just holding the area open. I feel around the edges of the incision, and my skin seems to go down if I push it. There is some movement available. I try to push the arms up a little, and they move slightly. As I do, my head hurts a little. There is a sickening pop. I realize the two sides of the two arms have come out of the incision. My neck has squeezed back together. I push up a little more, and the metallic arms stay up. I reach and feel my neck. The incision is still partially open. I don't know what to do, so I lightly push it shut. Fortunately, it still feels moist. Unfortunately, I realize I just used the word moist in my head. I hate that word.

My neck feels sore. As I move my arms, I no longer feel the pain I did moments ago. The two arms must have been pulling at the skin when I moved. Now I have to figure out my head. Does my neck hurt now? Am I paralyzed? If I move, is it going to kill me? I feel lost

97

for a moment and wonder if I should do anything. Maybe I should just wait for help? How long have I been here now? Why isn't help here yet? I hear *pops* again. Is that gunfire? What in the hell was going on?

I'm tired of waiting. Maybe it's better to die than lay on a table. I realize that my arm is not moving as easily because the IVs are still in it. I wonder if there's still anything in the IV. It could be that the IV is keeping me alive. I leave it alone. I reach up, and my right arm catches on the IV. I put it back down and reach with my left hand to the side of my head. There is a bracket holding my head. I can reach the other side as well, and there is a second bracket. With my hands, I study the brackets and realize there is an adjusting arm or bar on each side. I feel around on it and try to put pressure on the adjusting areas. It doesn't budge. I take a moment and breathe and realize maybe I should take out my breathing tube. I'm pretty sure that the regulated breathing tube is what has forced me to pass out. Then again, I'm not a doctor and have no real clue what I'm thinking. I leave that for last. In spite of the pain in my throat, I realize that if my head isn't free, the breathing tube isn't going to help. I reach up to the bar and put pressure up instead of down and feel it give way just a little. The pressure on my head is a little less. I take a moment longer and rest, then try again, and as I push up, the bar easily pushes away. My head can now move slightly.

There is a *pop pop pop*, and it is louder. I might be imagining it, but did I just see flashes of light? I push up on the apparatus holding my head. It moves up almost as though it was meant to. In my head I wonder what type of stupid thought that was. Of course, it's meant to move off of me.

I can move my head from side to side but only just a little. Is there pain in my neck? Did they finish the surgery, or had they even started it? If they're halfway through, moving could kill me or paralyze me at the very least. The *pops* are closer. I can see the flash. I recognize that flash. It's gunfire. I wonder what has happened. I know that I don't have a choice now. The flashes get faster, and I hear the door slam open.

I close my eyes and try to be quiet and breathe easy. Someone is in the room with me. How would I know if it's the good guy or the bad guy, or somebody completely different? I hear movement and the door pushing open and then closing. Are they still here? I hear clicking to my side and try to identify the sound as I try to stay calm and just lay there. I don't want to be a target. How many people are dead in this room? Why didn't I think of the dead people before now? I must be selfish.

I hear a few clicks and then a long click and snap. I remember the sound from a movie. It sounds like someone just chambered a round in a rifle. I try not to move. I peek and can see nothing. I hear the door again. It must be about six feet away. It might be ten. I'm not sure how I'll know for sure. I am laying on the table. My neck is closed. My head is free, but I have a tube down my throat feeding me oxygen. What was that movie, *Alien*? I still have IVs in my arm. I can move my legs, but they are wrapped in a sheet. Do I have clothes on? I'm not even sure. I open my eyes and look around the best that I can. I slide my head to the side, and my neck allows it. I see a man in a black suit looking out the operating room window. He has a rather intimidating-looking rifle. I'm sure many people would say it is an AR, but I don't think so. He's not looking at me at all.

He pushes out the door slightly, and I hear the loud *bang bang bang* instead of the *pops* I was hearing earlier. My ears are ringing. If I stay here, I'm going to die on this table. I look around the room and notice shadows moving above me. I see a man in the observation area with a helmet that says SWAT. I am both relieved and terrified. I look over to the side and see the gunman at the door. There is no clear shot from the observation room.

I look back at the man in the SWAT uniform, and he sees me. I swivel my eyes to where the gunman is, and my new best friend puts his finger to his lips and then nods to me. I see him ducking and moving, trying to find a way to get a shot. He can't get one. I look up at him and blink my eyes.

Reaching over, I pull out my IV, and it stings. The nice little tape they use is twisted now. I pull and wince and finally get the IV out. That's going to leave a bruise. My guardian Angel above me is shaking his head and hand 'no,' but I know what I must do. My IV is out, and I reach to my mouth and slowly pull out my breathing tube. This is something that I never thought I would ever be able to do. In response, I am introduced to an exciting level of different pain. I'm sure somewhere that some man might think this is kinky. I can tell you it is hurting like hell. It finally comes loose, and I throw it to the floor. I look over, and the gunman has turned to look at me. My eyes are filled with tears from pain and the stupidity of doing something this brave.

I reach inside with everything that I have and push my voice out. The first time it doesn't work. The second time I say in a horrid raspy voice, "Help me, please."

The gunman points his weapon at me.

"I thought you'd be dead by now. I left you to die when I killed that bastard who killed my wife."

The rifle was pointed right at me as he moved closer and closer.

"There wasn't gonna be any problems, huh? That's what they told me, and then they had the nerve to walk out and tell me there was a complication. My wife and I signed the papers trusting them, and there was nothing we were going to be able to do. Turned out there was nothing they could do for her at all, and she died just about like you are right now. The dumb ass on the floor was gonna kill you too, so I saved you. But I'm tired and just want everybody dead now."

The man starts to cry.

"It wasn't fair that they took her from me. She was my little buttercup and the only thing in this world that made me happy. They had to pay. Everybody has to pay now."

The rifle is pointed above me, and I see him slowly move it down. I see his eyes lock on mine and the sadness and anger flowing out of those eyes. I know this is the end of me. I wonder if the insurance covers death by bullets in surgery.

The gunman disappears backward with a large *bang*.

I look up, and above me, my guardian Angel looks down at me. A circular hole is cut in the glass. His rifle is still pointed out of it. I hear muffled voices as he talks into his radio, and then I see people begin to file in. Police and SWAT surround me, and I look up to see that the amphitheater window is now empty.

"Get a doctor in here!" I hear from the side.

I am surrounded in a moment by EMTs and nurses. They roll me out of the room, and I feel a needle in my arm.

I am in a bed. I can feel the sheets against my skin. The bed feels warm and inviting, and I have blankets on top of me. I open my eyes. The television is on. There is a news story playing. I see my face go past, but I can't hear it. There are flowers all around me. I'm not sure why. I don't have that many friends. A nurse walks in.

"You're awake," the nurse says. "A lot of people want to talk to you."

To the side, my brother walks up. "Damn girl, you're all over the news."

"What happened?" I ask in a raspy voice.

"What happened is that you distracted a killer, and the police put him down. He couldn't have gone down without you."

"What about the surgery?" I needed to know.

"Apparently, they were done before all the doctors got killed.

How do you feel?"

"I feel like I need a vacation." I smiled but remembered all I was feeling. "How many?"

"He killed your doctor and the three people in the operating room, then three police officers and the security guard."

"What now?" I asked.

"Go back to sleep, I'll be here, and we'll figure it out later."

I think about the surgery and everything I have been through. I wonder about my guardian Angel and then about the man's wife. I have many questions but mostly think about how afraid I had been, and I was still able to overcome it. I smile to myself for a moment and allow myself to relax. In moments I am asleep.

Ghost

"I'm telling you; I am a ghost." His voice echoed in my room. Brandon was always a little bit over the top, but this was a new one, even for him.

"Brandon, please, I'm trying to sleep." I barely yawned as I looked across the room and saw him sitting in the chair in front of my computer. "You don't look like a ghost; aren't ghosts supposed to be transparent or something?" I just wanted to sleep, and I didn't know why in the world Brandon had to start this today.

"I need your help." Brandon was pouting at me.

"If you're a ghost, why in the world would you need my help?" I was starting to wake up, and it was not helping the headache I went to bed with. I was studying too much and doing too many experiments for my science project.

"Well, no one else can see me." Brandon was pretty straightforward about this. "Since you can see me, I just need you to find my body so I can cross over or whatever the hell they call it."

"Didn't you and I watch a movie about this?" I was awake now, and this was not how I wanted to be. "Wasn't it a little girl or a guy or something like that?"

"That was a movie. This is reality. Sam, I need you to wake up so you can help me for a minute. I promise if we can find my body, I will leave you alone, and you can go back to sleep." Brandon was still pouting.

"No, I couldn't." I was getting pissed. "If we find your body, then you're dead, and I'm going to be awake explaining everything to the police and trying to figure out what in the hell is going on. Add to that that, I will be both pissed off and sad for losing you, and I won't get much sleep in the next several days. If it turns out this is some game, and you're trying to get me somewhere where we can screw around for a while, I still won't get any sleep. Why me, Brandon? I mean, we were best friends for a long time, and we're still good friends, but you don't hang out with me anymore. You've been screwing around with goofballs, which probably killed you, if you are a ghost."

"You got that right," Brandon laughed. "Those idiots are what got me killed, and they just left me."

"All right, tell me a story." I sat up in my bed and put on my T-shirt and the pants I was wearing last night. They felt heavy, and I tapped the pockets to realize the lighters and measurement tools were still in my pocket for my science project.

"It's not a very complicated story." Brandon looked out the window. "It was just a few miles away from here. The guys I was with wanted to go into this house that they said was haunted. It's a scary-looking house but not as bad as some of them. Their idea was to piss the ghost off and have a few laughs. Why in the world would anyone want to piss a ghost off? We went to the house and got in easily. It quickly got creepy. Random noises separated us, and then it became pretty apparent that the house was not only haunted but also methodically trying to take each one of us. By take, I mean kill."

"Okay, I'll bite." I bet I sounded irritated. "Why in the world would a ghost want to kill people? Or was it the house? Then the question is, why in the world would a house want to kill people?"

"Don't you get it?" Brandon was sullen. "It's like the house or the ghost or whatever eats people to make it stronger. When the five of us idiots got in there, it was weak, but as it eats people, it gets stronger. It told me it had been almost 100 years since anyone had been inside the house that it could kill. That's why it killed all five of us. Those idiots tried to run, but the house was too fast for them, and just went ahead and killed them right there. Then it got me. It told me that the only way our souls would be released would be if someone found us. I tried to go to the police and home. I tried everything and couldn't get anyone to see me but you. I figure you must be the one to break this curse so we can be free of the house. I'm not sure why, though.”

“Let me get the rest of my clothes on.” I was still pretty pissed as I dug out a fresh pair of socks and a sweatshirt.

It was dark outside when we walked out onto my street. I should have looked at it, Brandon, and asked why he didn't walk through the door, but it seemed that he was walking with me, talking to me, and being just like Brandon. The house was only a few blocks away, so we decided to walk. I was wearing my tennis shoes, cargo pants, and a sweatshirt, while Brandon still wore the combat boots, black pants, black shirt, and black duster he had become known for. Things like his fashion choices created a rift between us as he just wanted to be different and nothing else. That's what bothered me most. I was a friend to somebody I barely knew. All Brandon ever wanted was attention, but he and his friends didn't stand for anything.

As we walked up the street, I recognized the house. I had driven by it hundreds of times. It was old, Victorian, and way out of repair. As we walked up to the gate, it swung open, which would have freaked me out if my once best friend hadn't told me he was dead already tonight. I was ready for anything. We walked into the yard, and it reminded me of every scary movie I ever saw, leading me to believe that I was the idiot about to be eaten by the vampire zombies, or whatever. This oughta be good.

“I'm not sure where I am.” Brandon looked a little lost. “I thought I was laying right here in front of the house, but I guess I was moved.”

“So now we get to play hokey pokey with the house until we find you?”

“I guess we're supposed to go inside.” Brandon began walking up the steps, causing the wood to creak.

“Maybe we should go get a few more people,” I said; “there

is, after all, safety in numbers."

"All you have to do is see me, and it's over. You can go home and go back to bed." Brandon implored.

I walked up the stairs, and they creaked just as they had a few minutes ago. The door cracked open as I pushed it, and I felt like an idiot for even being there. Still, I did grow up with Brandon, so maybe I needed to do this for myself. That's when it got weird.

I was standing in the giant atrium just after walking inside the door and suddenly felt dizzy. I looked around the room and saw a stack of bodies sitting in the corner. I recognized them as Brandon's friends simply because of the boots, pants, and dusters that Brandon was wearing. They looked like rejects from the *Matrix* that were too slow for their slow-motion part. I felt woozy and wanted to leave.

Brandon walked over to the stack of bodies and looked back at me. "I don't know where I am, they are here, but I'm not."

I couldn't concentrate. I grabbed onto the wall to steady myself and looked over at Brandon. He smiled a strange smile.

"It is about time." Brandon was speaking out loud. "I told you I would bring somebody back. I'll get you more, but you can't just wait around to pull that dizzy shit."

I was stumbling a little, but my mind comprehended that I was in some sort of trap. "What's going on?"

"Easy, my ex-friend." Brandon came up and pushed me a little. "The house needed somebody and took my friends, but I made a deal. If I brought others back, my life gets spared. I knew you would come; you always were sappy. Why in the world would you help me? You were always the goody two shoes while I had to struggle."

I was trying to focus, but it was hard. I looked around the room for anything to help me. The floor creaked, and I realized Brandon just wasn't a ghost. Ghosts don't make floors creak, at least not in any movie I had ever seen. "You're not a ghost."

"You're right." Brandon was smug. "I cut a deal as a human to deliver more humans. I figured I could come up with at least 10 or 15 rather than just little old me. The house was intrigued, I suppose, so I was all in. The house even says it will give my friends back if I get enough dimwits for the exchange."

"You made a deal with the house?" I was struggling to stay awake, and I guess the house was trying to make sure I embraced that sleep. "Doesn't the house know how much you lie?"

"It's a house," Brandon grinned; "if I only get five and get rid of five people I don't want to see, that's a win for both of us."

"How did you know you could even talk to the house?" I was trying to stall and move towards the door.

"I didn't. I just yelled it out loud, and it let me go."

I didn't think; I just screamed. "I want out!!!"

Brandon laughed at me, but I was feeling better as I kept screaming, "He is lying to you as he lied to me!!!"

Brandon looked around and rushed towards me. He struck me in the face, and I fell to the ground.

"You are not going to mess this up for me." Brandon was furious. "I will kill you myself."

I began to work my way to my knees when I saw him swing at me with his leg. I twisted out of the way, and he slipped and fell. I wanted to laugh as the situation was very much like how a real fight goes. Movies usually depict fights as some grandiose dance but missing and falling was more realistic. As I stood up, my pocket clunked against me. I remembered with clarity my science experiment and the simple flares I had mixed in the lab. Brandon was trying to get up. I got up faster and pushed him down. I was feeling a little clearer, but my head was still muddled as I pulled one of the flares out of my pocket. The object was to create a signaling device that could be carried anywhere safely. To do this, I combined several chemicals to create a quick-start short-burn magnesium flare. The initial flames were like that of a match, but once the magnesium started, it would burn for 30 seconds, and nothing could put it out. I pulled the string on the flair in my pocket, and nothing happened. I was frustrated as I had tested these hundreds of times before. Brandon was getting up.

I reached into my pocket and pulled out the remaining five flares I had made for my project. I was running out of time and pulled the string on another. I was rewarded instantly with a bright red flame followed by an even brighter white flame just a second later. I threw the flare to the floor, then pulled the string on another, and another. I had two left that I threw back into my pocket as Brandon struggled to his feet. I ran to the door and was surprised that it was open.

As I ran outside, I saw the bright flames burning inside. More flames started to erupt until the entire house was engulfed. I was on the street but could feel the flames, and the warmth of that flame lapped at me. I didn't know how to feel. Brandon used to be a friend, but this was weird. I felt sleepy for a moment.

I jumped up, and I was in my bed. Was any of it real? I grabbed my jacket and my flares we were all there. None had been burned. I thought about it for a moment and wondered why I was thinking about Brandon. I decided to try to call him. After all, it had been a while.

I dialed his number. The phone rang and a voice answered, "Hello?"

"Hey Brandon, long time no talk," I said.

"I'm sorry Brandon isn't available," the voice said; "who is this?"

"It's Sam." I was a little confused. "Sam Ketchum."

"Well, Sam," the voice began, "Brandon was found in a house last night in a coma. We're trying to figure out what happened, but it looks like some type of holiday prank gone wrong. Where were you last night?"

I was a little taken aback. "I was in class and then asleep. I dreamed about Brandon and just wanted to check on him."

"We have your number from the phone. I will have someone call you and ask a few questions," the voice said.

"Wait a second." This night was just weird. "Is Brandon okay?"

"We will let you know," the voice said.

I hung up the phone. It took me just a minute to get dressed, and I put on my jacket with the flares still in my pocket. I walked to the house from my recent dream, and there it was. The house was smoking, and multiple fire trucks and ambulances swarmed the area. A yellow police line surrounded the scene, with numerous officers keeping people back. I walked to the line and watched Brandon loaded into an ambulance. He was wearing exactly what he was in my dream. Behind it all, the house still smoldered, and I wondered how much of my dream might have been real.

Channel Surfing

I can say without question that I would much rather live life than watch television. It's annoying though, because I watch television far more than I should. It's hard to get out and be in the middle of everything. After COVID, the world seemed to be a mess, and people seemed to be messier, period.

I spent my evenings watching television and trying to find something that wasn't completely ridiculous. As I scanned channels one evening, I came across a weird channel at 9997. The channel was blank, and black turned to gray and then gray to black. I sat there staring at it for a moment, and my mind began to wander. On the screen, images started to appear. I was not paying attention until I realized the images were moving, and it was a woman cooking dinner.

She was wearing a blue T-shirt that had *Diesel* imprinted on the center. She also wore jeans, and as I paid more attention, I saw "Levi Straus" on a patch on the back of her jeans. She moved back and forth, focusing on the counter, and the view came closer and closer. I was unsure why I was so intrigued by this image until she turned around. There in front of me was Ruth, my girlfriend from high school. Well, the girl I wanted to be my girlfriend, well, my crush. I couldn't lie to myself. I think she knew I liked her, but I never got past the "handshake and a hug" stage. She moved on, and I lost track of her. Now I was a pitiful software developer in my late 20s, and she looked incredible as she cooked and made dinner. The camera followed her, like any good reality show, and she walked to the table. It was set for one. Why? She should be happily married by now. A phone number appeared at the bottom of the screen. I was unsure what to do, but I grabbed my phone and called.

On the screen, I saw her answer. She said, "Hello," and I could see and hear it.

"Hi," I stuttered; "Is this Ruth?"

She was speaking on TV and in my ear. "Yes, this is Ruth. Who is this?"

"I'm not sure if you will remember me, but this is Jason, Jason Wilson, from Jimmy Creek?"

On the screen, she looked shocked but smiled, "Jason?" she sat down. "How did you get my number?"

"I don't think you would believe me if I told you," I said. "You wouldn't happen to be on a reality show, would you?"

"No, I hate reality shows," she was relaxed on screen. "Are you on a reality show?"

"No, I hate them too." I was wondering how this was happening, "I was wondering if you would like to get dinner sometime. I don't know if you're with somebody, but I have thought about you since high school and can't get you out of my head. If you can't, it's okay, but..."

Ruth broke in almost immediately, "I would love to get dinner with you. I've thought about you too. I just got out of a divorce about a year and a half ago. I'm learning how to like myself, and I realized the people that were important in my life I never got to see. One of my regrets was never going out with you."

I was nearly blushing, but I took this as an impressive and fantastic sign. "Anytime you want to, I'm ready. I realize that sounds eager, but I've been thinking about you a lot, and it seems fate has given us this possibility. If you're interested, pick a night, and I'll be there. You'll have to tell me where there is, but I will be there."

"Well, how did you get my phone number?"

"I can tell you that at dinner and anything else you want to know." I was giddy.

"Tomorrow night, then. Pick me up at six. Call my number tomorrow, and I'll tell you my address."

111

I was excited, but the excitement wasn't over. We talked for over two hours about everything and nothing. I felt like I had missed out on a big part of my life, and the entire time I spoke to her, I could see her on the television. It felt a little weird, but I wasn't going to say anything. After all, this was my dream, and I didn't want it to end. When I hung up the phone, the picture went away. Before me, a flashing grey and black screen showed nothing, and no indication that anything else had ever been there. Still, I was excited and overjoyed with the possibility of seeing Ruth and going out on a date. As I watched her, she was excited while she talked to me, and I was just as excited. I went to bed and couldn't think about anything else.

The next day I was lost at work for quite a while. Things kept coming my way, and with releases and bugs being shoved on top of me, I became increasingly irritated. Then I remembered that I was going out with Ruth shortly. I laughed and smiled and was more than excited as the day ended.

It was four o'clock. I rushed home, got ready, and called Ruth. She answered immediately, and it was apparent she was as excited as I was. We quickly decided to meet at Ruth Chris and choose how our night would go based on our dinner. We would both take an Uber and make it up from there.

I was at Ruth Chris ten minutes early. I sat out at the front with my legs shaking in my business casual clothes. I was trying to look cool but I was nervous as hell. My foot tapped on the floor so fast that, at one point, the maître dee looked at me and raised an eyebrow. I wasn't embarrassed, and at three minutes till six, Ruth walked in. She was stunning, and I had no idea what to say. I stuttered and was lost until I finally said, "You look beautiful."

Ruth smiled at me. "You're not half bad, yourself."

The maître dee walked up and asked if I was finally ready to be seated. "Yes, of course."

We walked to a small table off to the side. The table was

perfect, and as we sat and talked, I was lost in the eyes of this beautiful woman I had nearly forgotten. I would never have forgotten her, but I was impressed and excited.

"How did you get my phone number? I just got a new phone," Ruth asked.

"You wouldn't believe me if I told you," I said.

"Try me," Ruth pressed.

"Well, I was channel surfing last night and found this weird channel at the end. I wasn't really paying attention, but my mind drifted to you, and suddenly I could see you on the screen. I watched you make dinner in your *Diesel* shirt and carry that over to the table, where you sat alone until I called. I guess it's my fault because I was thinking about calling you and suddenly the number was on the screen. I thought it was a reality show or something, but I think my television thought it was mystical or was trying to be a dating app. I don't know. I know this sounds weird, but I'm glad it happened because I'm sitting with you right now."

Ruth looked at me sideways. She glanced at the other tables and then back at me, "You are not kidding, are you?"

"No, and no; I don't wanna lie to you. It would have been easier to lie, but I always found it's easier to tell the truth, and deal with whatever."

"I appreciate you telling me the truth. I'm not sure if I believe it."

"That's okay. I'm not sure I believe it either." I was being serious.

We spent two hours eating, laughing, and having some of the best steaks on the planet. There are only a few places with better steaks than Ruth Chris, which are often hard to get to. As the night continued, we didn't slow down, and eventually, it was evident that the staff was trying to run us off. We had capitalized on a prime table spot for over three hours. I did not feel bad at all, but I left a good tip.

As we were standing outside in the lobby, I called for an Uber, and Ruth was also calling. Then she hung up her phone. "I'd like to see your TV if that's okay?"

"Sure." I made a face that rivaled the giggliest look in any movie. Five minutes later, and a fast Uber driver after that, and we were at my house. We went up, I unlocked the door, and we went inside.

As we walked into the house, Ruth grabbed me, pushed me against the wall, and then began kissing me. This was intense and had never happened to a geek like me. A few moments later, Ruth pulled away and said, "Wow, we should have done that in high school."

We walked into the living room. Ruth sat down on my couch, and soon we were kissing again. There was a lot of intensity, a lot of heavy petting, and a lot of stimulating feelings. I felt like I was 16 again, but I wasn't, and we were about to go too far for a first date.

We both slowed down, and it was soft petting and kissing for a while. Ruth was curled up inside my arm, and I must admit I was in heaven. This was something I had dreamed of. This was something I had wanted. It was then that Ruth asked about the television. I turned it on and tuned it to that magical station that didn't seem to have any purpose. The television acted just like it did the day before. It flashed gray and black and didn't show anything on that unique channel that had shown me Ruth.

"I'm not sure how it works. This is what it did yesterday. Then suddenly, it started showing you. Maybe it was only meant to work once."

I scanned the channels back and forth a few times and got nowhere. There really wasn't much to do, so we kissed again and spent more time kissing. Finally, Ruth stood up and took me into my bedroom. I looked at her dumbfounded.

"Look, I've been married, and I'm certain you're not a virgin, and I know that I really want this."

For the next two hours, we existed only in each other's arms and in each other. I doubted anyone could understand how happy I was. I was over the moon. We fell asleep in each other's arms and woke up at 4:00 AM, naked and sweaty, and both of us had to pee.

We were both wide awake and now were holding each other and just being lost in the moment. We both put on my clothes. I put on a long shirt and shorts, and Ruth took one of my sweatshirts, and we went out to the couch and talked, and talked some more. At 5:00 AM, we turned on the television, and Ruth showed me her favorite channel, the *ID* channel. We watched a program about a particularly gruesome unsolved serial killer that was still active. The killer found people who were alone, usually a single white female, and was brutal to them before dressing them up and setting them up like a dollhouse in their homes or apartments. He always finished it with a red ribbon tying their hair up in a pretty little knot. I was fascinated and had never seen anything like this. Ruth had seen the episode, and part of the way through it, she reached over and kissed me again, and as we were holding each other, she hit the last channel on the remote.

There it was. My mystery channel flashed black and gray and black and gray and then suddenly static. We looked at the television because it was different, and as it began to focus, the scene before us was gruesome. A woman was struggling as a middle-aged man was brutalizing her. The actual footage was so crisp that I felt I could reach through the screen and see it. The woman screamed, and it sounded like the piercing scream of a banshee or a wailing woman full of sorrow. We both shuddered. The man tied the woman to the bed and had a series of knives and instruments. It was one of the most horrible things I had ever seen, and then I saw the red ribbon on the side. I pointed it out to Ruth, and she sat up almost immediately.

"I wonder if this is live and where it is?"

I had no idea. "I'm not sure, but if it's like when I was talking to you, it is real-time."

On the bottom of the screen, a series of numbers appeared, followed by an address. The address was only six blocks away. I picked up my phone and dialed 911. I quickly told the dispatcher I had been outside that particular address, and something seemed wrong. There was screaming. I told the dispatcher I had come home to make the call because I didn't have my cell phone with me at the time. They asked for my name in a moment and then hung up and said they would look into it.

We watched as the man cut off the woman's clothes. She sobbed and shook her head, pulling on her arms and trying to get free. She was held fast but didn't give up. He touched her everywhere when she was completely naked, and you could tell it was destroying her from the inside out. It had been almost five minutes, but I saw what I thought was a flicker of light near the window. With a sudden smash, the door fell in, and two officers rushed into the room. The man stood and held a gun in his hand. The officers fired, and the man fired as well. There was smoke and mist, and we could barely see. Ruth was holding on to me so tight that I thought my arm was going to go to sleep. A few minutes later, Ruth let go when she saw the officers helping the woman up and the serial killer dead on the ground.

Ruth looked at me and grabbed me tight. "We saved that woman?"

"That was intense." I was still pumped up with adrenaline waiting for the next moment to come.

Ruth kissed me, and as we held each other, I saw from the corner of my eye that the television began flashing grey and black again. I wondered how long this station would stay with me and if the rest of the world had access, or if it was just me. As I held Ruth, I was thankful for whatever gift we had, even if it never came again.

The Party

"It's just a party," Val was reassuring me. He had a way about him that calmed me down. When we first met, I used to think that his gaze was hypnotic. Now I knew I was just overly in love with this man. "We've been to lots of parties together."

"It's been months since we've been in a crowd. Crowds mean people and people can be so annoying. They're all so unpredictable. It's not like we have to be here. Let's meet with everybody one at a time. It'll give us more time to get to know them and a lot more privacy."

"We're new to the area and it only makes sense that we would be invited. You've been invited into this awesome house, and we are gonna have a great time. I'm sure there's going to be great food. I'm also sure we'll get a dance and enjoy each other, more than anything."

"I intend to enjoy all the people, but you know me. I'm always worried we're going to find somebody we shouldn't, or that we're going to have a less than perfect time, or that someone is going to walk away and think that we are horrible people. We're not horrible, we just aren't the same as everybody else. I guess when you've been in love as long as we have everyone else seems kind of lame."

We walked up to the door of the easily 7,000 square foot home and heard the music through the walls. It was an upbeat song from the 80s and they were going at it big time. I remember dancing to this tune in the 80s and I'm sure Val has pleasant memories as well. He and I have been through a lot, and it was going to keep getting better. We just had to keep our heads on straight and hold on to each other. I guess we also had to protect our hearts; we had both been hurt a lot before we met. Val glanced at me and smiled, then knocked the door.

The bright lights suddenly glared on the porch and the door

opened. The man answering the door was dressed as pirate and we both smiled as he said, "You must be Val and Eva. Welcome to the neighborhood, come on in."

We were both cautious as we walked into the house. There was commotion everywhere and people walking from side to side so fast you would think they actually had a purpose. We knew better. We were used to people being less than perfect and being so unaware and self-absorbed that they never noticed anything.

"I love your costumes," our host said; "I haven't seen 70s garb in a while. You look really mod. My name is Chip. I hope you enjoy our little party. We are a pretty close-knit group."

I walked up to our host and was very flirtatious. I played with the curl that was barely underneath the bandana of his pirate costume. He gulped in response. I ran my hand down his face ever so softly and looked down at his chest. "Hey pirate," I laughed, "I like your sword."

"Umm, yeah," he was a stammering mess. "Why don't you come into the main room and meet everyone."

We walked through the hallway with our host in the lead to a large recreation room filled with people. Music was playing as loud as it could without violating some ridiculous HOA policy. Our host walked to the front of the room. He turned off the music.

"Quiet down everyone. I'd like to introduce Val and Eva. All of you know my name is Chip, but please take a moment and introduce yourselves to our newest neighbors. They are welcome in our hearts and in our homes."

I looked at Val and smiled.

The next 30 minutes were difficult. I met a series of people that would make your head spin, and it felt like my head was spinning. From the twins that still lived in the house together at 35 years old to the oldest residents of the area, the Masons. At 71 they had been married for 50 years. They had lived a good life and Melba Mason was sure to talk your ear off. I spent five minutes trying to get away as she told me about everyone and everything that she had ever done. I felt sorry for the list of men she rattled off because she had done a lot before she turned 21, and still remembered them all. Val and I met in the center of the room.

"There are 20 people here," I said. I have talked to 12. None of them have any children or anyone waiting at home for them. Six of them have dogs. The rest came to this community to be without children and without responsibility. For the most part, the entire group is about as threatening as a hamster in a blender."

"I spoke to the other eight," Val looked around; "they too are pretty lame. Bill, the big guy in the corner, used to be a sheriff. If you look at the belly on him, you probably wouldn't believe it. He's been retired for 10 years and makes birdhouses as a hobby. What do you think?"

"I think it's time," I said. "I don't think there's any possibility of anything to worry about."

I went to the front of the room and turned the music down. There were three couples dancing at the time and they immediately looked at me. The rest of the group had settled in and were talking at different clusters of couches and chairs. It took a moment to get everyone's attention.

"Can I have your attention please?" I looked around the room and counted in my head. All twenty were here. "Thanks everyone. Val and I are so pleased to be here and so happy that you invited us into your home. This has been one of the most spectacular nights that we will ever have. I want to thank you all in advance for all you're about to give us."

The people in the room turned and looked at each other as they weighed the words that I had said. As all eyes were on me no one noticed as Val used an ice pick at the back of each of the first

119

nine people's heads. They stood for a second and then began to fall to the ground or slumped in their seats before anyone noticed. Val was so precise with the implement that he stopped major brain function without stopping the autonomous brain from working. What that meant is as each body fell, it was almost like it was in a coma. Val was able to pith six more before people turn around. Five of them remained and as one of them began to swing at Val he deftly ducked and pithed his brain as well. Four remained, and as they looked at Val, I grabbed the nearest one to me from behind and sunk my fangs deep into their jugular vein. I sucked hard as I felt the venom push its way into their body, paralyzing them and allowing me to feed without interruption. I felt their body go limp and released them just as the second turned and swung towards me. Val had the big man by the throat. His fangs were sunk deep into the man's neck. I stepped toward the woman who was swinging at me and screaming, and pulled her into me. I felt her breasts against mine and it felt good. She was flailing but her arms were outside of mine and as I held her, I sunk my teeth into her neck and began injecting my venom into her while draining her blood. She moaned and pulled my head closer into her neck and I reveled in the taste of her life. The last man standing was Chip. He was shaking and looking at both of us in disbelief. Seventeen bodies lay on the floor, and we held two. Both of us looking at him while we fed on their lives.

I started to drop the woman, but she would not let me go. She urged me on and was lost in the venom induced rapture that I had caused. I let her go and she cried. She put her hands between her legs, squealing in raw delight. She rocked side to side like a junkie who needed another fix but all she wanted was to feel me taking her life a little at a time.

Val dropped the big man. He looked down at the woman, "She's a lively one."

"I thought about keeping her," I was serious. "She is very passionate and would be a good companion for us both."

Chip was backing away slowly towards the back door.

"Come on Chip you can't get away," Val said. "We can do this the easy way or the hard way."

"How about we don't do it at all?" Chip was looking at both of us.

"It's okay Chip," I looked him in the eye; "I would love for you to show me your sword."

Chip gulped again and his back was now against the sliding glass door.

"You don't want me," he begged; "I would taste bad anyway. I don't eat right and have high cholesterol. I probably eat too much garlic too. That wouldn't be very good for you."

I reached the side of Chip and traced my hand down his face again. He cringed at my touch. I pulled his head closer to me and brought him in for a kiss. I could still taste the blood on my lips from the woman who was still writhing on the floor. My tongue traced along his lips, and he tried to pull away, but I didn't let him move. I kissed him and forced my tongue into his mouth. It only took a moment, and he was kissing me back with equal fervor. I let go and he held me and forced his tongue into my mouth. His tongue grazed one of my fangs and I tasted his blood. He tasted so grand. I put my leg around his and he pushed towards me hard, trying to kiss me even more while our tongues fought for control. He slowly pulled away and looked me in the eyes with defeat and incredible lust. He bared his neck and looked at me. He was giving himself to me. I kissed him and did not bite him.

"Chip," I whispered. Val heard it as well and smiled at me. "What would you do to be with me?"

"I would do anything to be with you Eva, you're the most beautiful woman I've ever seen."

"If I let you have me, will you help us find another subdivision like this one?"

"I would help you find anything you wanted."

"It doesn't bother you that Val and I are together?"

"No, I just would love to be yours."

"Why don't you go upstairs and get cleaned up. You have a wet spot in your pants. We'll clean up down here."

Val and I fed. There were 18 people and we drained them all. We kept Chip and Irene alive. Irene served us day and night and we enjoyed our time with her. We were right to keep her because her passion seemed to be without limit. Chip helped us sell his house and he found another subdivision with no ties and no children. Chip had his way with me hundreds of times and is the happiest he has ever been. He and Irene moved in together in the new subdivision. They're throwing a party next week. I hope you can join us there.

The Edges

Alexandra stared out the window into the dull rainy afternoon. She looked out across the warehouse district and felt a chill inside, knowing that she was probably alone right now. Alexandra's roommate, Karen, was gone for two weeks in Europe. One of her classes offered her the opportunity to study abroad and she dove at the chance. She had no boyfriend and no ties in the world except for Alexandra. Alexandra had no one right now.

Alexandra's challenging life made having any friends sometimes difficult, and more often those friends did not understand the handicap she had, and the struggles it took just to walk across a room. That was before. Six months ago, Alexandra found a sword in a secondhand shop. She actually didn't find the sword but instead, found an ornate case with a unique puzzle box on the outside. As she was cleaning the case, she understood how the puzzle worked and suddenly was the owner of a majestic sword. Mere hours after discovering the sword, Alexandra was locked in a fight for her friend's life. While defending herself, the sword slid through one of her attackers, turning them to dust. In the process, Alexandra regained her strength and her disease was now gone. Even her roommate, Karen, did not remember that evening. Her boyfriend at the time had given her an overdose of fentanyl and as her boyfriend attacked them both, Alexandra used the newfound power of the sword to take the boyfriend's life and save Karen.

Alexandra considered all that happened, and it sounded like she was a horrible person. She killed three people and she felt no remorse for it. The sword itself was now bound to her and she liked it. A short time ago, while searching a library and ancient texts for clues, Alexandra found a librarian who had another sword. The librarian told her there were numerous swords of power and assumed that Alexandra had one, in particular. Alexandra learned that day that she could call the sword to her from anywhere and in doing so, learned that her sword was the sword of Fury. The librarian who had lived many lifetimes using her sword was fearful after learning that Alexandra had the sword of Fury, and avoided the conflict. She was looking for the sword of Balance and she did not name her sword. She did state there were seven swords and Alexandra only knew the names of two. Alexandra also learned that day, that for hundreds of years, the librarian, Marjorie, was eliminating all record of the seven.

Alexandra continued her search through old texts and libraries but could find no reference of the sword or any other sword with special abilities or their origins. Alone in her warehouse apartment, she watched the rain and considered what she should do next.

Alexandra's phone rang and she saw that it was Karen calling her. Karen had been gone a week now and called her every few days just to check in.

"Hello?"

"I think you need to get over here," Karen sounded kind of frantic.

"Are you here in town?"

"No silly, I'm still in Italy. I'm in a small town in Tuscan area. I was looking around and I found this bookstore. It looks like it's been around since Zeus was throwing lightning bolts. Anyway, I was looking through the books for something to bring back to you, and I found a series of leather-bound books that have hand carvings of your sword on the front of them. It also looks like there is a whole section, maybe hundreds of books, on different swords. They are little expensive but the old man running the shop is willing to bargain. Is there any way you could fly over? That way you could get what you wanted, and I wouldn't be spending a bunch of money on things they might not let me take out of the country anyway?"

"Send me a text to where you are. Where you're staying, at least. I will head that way in the morning. The last time I was in Italy it was about an eight-hour flight, so I should be there by tomorrow night."

"And then you and I will get to go shopping together once more." Karen was laughing.

"Hey Karen," Alexandra was a little concerned, "I love you and all so stay safe. If anybody starts asking questions, tell them you don't know anything and just like the pictures. After my run in with the librarian, I really don't want you to get in the middle of it all."

"I'll be careful, bye," Karen laughed as the line went dead.

Alexandra stood and walked over to her bedroom. Inside, on the wall, was the puzzle box that contained the sword of Fury. It was funny that she was concerned about someone taking it since she could call it to herself with a thought. Still, there was no way that she could get this sword through customs, so it had to stay. Alexandra packed her bag and made sure she packed her cane. Even though she could now easily walk she could not explain how someone with her condition could ever be healed. With that in mind, she had to continuously feign her malady.

Alexandra then took the time to book her flight. She used an app and saved quite a bit of money. She wondered if this would be a wild goose chase or if she would finally understand a little bit about how she was changed. The flight left at 5:00 AM, which allowed her an evening to rest.

Instead of resting, Alexandra paced the top floor apartment of her warehouse. The warehouse below was quiet at night, but her mind was not. Ever since she found the sword, her luck had changed, and her life had changed. The frustration and anger that she felt because of her disease was still there but she had nothing at which to direct it. The warehouse beneath her had been more successful lately, and they had finally caught up on their rent. For the first time in a long time, Alexandra had money in the bank. School had been relatively easy and the only bump she experienced was when

125

Marjorie challenged her. It was on that day she found that her sword would be in her hand anytime she needed it.

The warehouse apartment had several rooms. The two largest were set up as bedrooms for her and Karen, with a central area in between them. There were also numerous bathrooms, two kitchens, and a lot of empty space or storage space, depending on how it was used. Right now, Alexandra walked up and down through all of the areas, running through some of it, as the clock ticked. Her excitement had her mind in overdrive. If she had her own plane, she would have already been flying it. The world seemed so slow since she found the sword. The world, in reality, was not slow. By ten o'clock she was finally feeling a little less antsy. Alexandra laid down in her bed with an alarm set for 2:30 AM. This would allow her time to get there and be ready for her flight.

Alexandra fell asleep. Her dreams were filled with swirling swords and naked edges slicing through steel and bone as if they were water. She dreamed that she was fighting a man in a suit of armor. His sword was twice the size of hers and he was relentlessly hammering at her. Each time she blocked and parried he would step away and be missed only by an inch. Alexandra gave no quarter, and he took none. It seemed like they were fighting forever and twisting out of each other's way by only a fraction. The man in the suit of armor stopped and slammed his sword into the ground. As he removed his helmet it was not a "he" at all, but instead, was Karen. She picked up the long sword and brought it down in a brutal strike, but Alexandra was quicker and caught the blade in her quillons, then twisted only slightly as the quillon entered the armor. Alexandra cried as she saw Karen's face melt to dust in the now empty armor.

Alexandra woke in a sweat thinking of Karen melting before her. Karen was her friend and had been since they were very young. This was her mind trying to explain something to her and it was not something easy. What was she missing? She sat in her bed for a few moments and looked up as Karen swung the huge broadsword down upon her. She screamed and sat up where she had been asleep. In her hand was the sword of Fury waiting for her command to protect her.

Alexandra was panting and her mind was a flurry. She was slowing down, breathing, trying to relax, then her alarm went off. Maybe it was time for her to go to Italy on vacation. She was way too keyed up. She concentrated on the sword, and it disappeared. She knew it was back in its box waiting for the next time she would call.

No one could describe Alexandra as high maintenance. Her reputation for having a ridiculously short-fuse temper was well known around campus. Along with that reputation came the statements wondering if she had just rolled out of bed and rushed to class. Today was no different. Alexandra showered and cleaned up but spent no extra time on making herself look any better than she could have looked. She was comfortable within her own skin. Facing every day for years knowing that the next day she might not be able to walk, or that she could die, had given her a pure acceptance of herself. Even with the gift the sword had given her, she still held on to the idea that she was who she was, and few others mattered. Alexandra packed light, with just a backpack and an oversized purse. The backpack held her clothes while the purse had her laptop and a few other items. She knew she had to travel light to continue with the ruse of her infirmity. Even though no one would know her, she could not afford to give away the fantastic gift she had been given.

The Uber ride was uneventful. The driver, whose name was Ted, introduced himself and offered her a water. She was in the back of a very nice Chevy Impala and Ted did not talk much. That was fine with her. When she arrived at the airport, she, her luggage, and her cane checked in and went to the International gate with no issue. The airline offered her a wheelchair, but she said since it was a direct flight it wouldn't be necessary. An hour later the flight boarded, and an hour after that they were in the air.

Alexandra was not a fan of flying. This flight was very smooth, and the airline had upgraded her to first class for no apparent reason other than her malady. This was something that normally didn't happen, but she wasn't going to look a gift horse in the mouth. Instead, she rode the plane comfortably and enjoyed the free champagne.

Seven hours passed and she was landing in the heart of Italy. After landing in Pisa, she took a bus to a little village called Spignana. The trip was uneventful, and she soon arrived at the Airbnb address that Karen gave her. The villa looked as though it should be in a movie. It was extremely well kept and recently painted. It could have been two years or 200 years old. The architecture was amazing, and Alexandra could have spent a lot of time looking, if not for the setting sun. She stopped for a moment, looked out over the horizon, and watched the sun set over the western sky. The absolute beauty of the countryside added to the feeling of utter and complete peace. This was how life should be. Alexandra knocked at the door.

Karen opened the door, and her expression went from mundane to overjoyed in a matter of seconds. She walked out the door, grabbed Alexandra in a big hug, and held her tight. "I know I haven't been gone long but I have missed you and your sunny disposition."

"It's obvious that the Tuscan wine has gotten to you," Alexandra quipped.

Karen laughed. "I have so much to tell you. Some of it is absolutely amazing and some of it is just what I am normally. You're going to be so happy."

"What did you do?" Alexandra was strangely suspicious or perhaps it was not so strange. Karen put her into unique situations several times because of her over-trusting, lack of sensibilities.

"I didn't do anything this time. I spent some time looking at the books I was talking about, and I think you'll be interested. Most of it is way over my head but the books are hundreds of years old. I did go to the library and looked around as well, and they have an antique book section that is even larger than most we have seen.

Think about it, this little village has a library with an antique book section. Some of the books are exactly what you're looking for."

Alexandra considered for just a moment. "How late is everything open?"

"Well, they won't be open now. It seems like everything rolls up after dark and everyone is either at a bar, eating, or trying to decide which bar they're going to or what they will eat. It's very different over here."

"Where is the rest of your class?" Alexandra was curious since she was there with 19 other people.

"We are spread out around the city. Well, this is really a village. Anyway, we are spread out but meet every morning at 9:00 AM and every night at 4:00 PM. That keeps us on track, and we can tell each other whatever we need to keep going. It has worked pretty good so far."

"What was this class again?" Alexandra wasn't sure what kind of class came to Italy and spread out in a small town in the middle of nowhere looking for nothing in particular.

"Oh, you know, it's Classical Art 306. It centers around finding beauty in both the old and the new. We are supposed to be looking at the contrasts between ancient times and current times."

"Is there anything to eat around here?" Alexandra suddenly realized just how hungry she was. It had been a long flight and she wasn't hungry during the flight. The time shift would also have an effect on her. Moving over eight hours threw her body off because of the changes in daylight.

"Yeah, there's a little bar down the street that has food. There are a lot of locals there, but it will be just fine."

Alexandra heard her stomach growl. "I think it's time to go visit the bar." She was famished, and it was absolutely necessary that she gets some calories before morning. She had some breakfast bars in her pack but that would not be good enough. "Do you think they'll have a cheeseburger?"

"I doubt it, but they might have some meatballs," Karen laughed.

"I'm surprised you haven't gotten into any trouble," Alexandra said as Karen closed the door, and they began walking down the cobblestone street.

"It's not for a lack of trying. The professor is a real bore, and this entire class revolves around impressing them. I've tried to get things rocking a little bit but we're also in the middle of nowhere, in the town that time forgot. The bar we're going to as a jukebox and the most recent rock song was sung by Elvis."

"I'm sure that's not 100% true," Alexandra chuckled; "you just haven't found a series of bad boys to ruin your life yet."

"No, I've told you over and over I'm done with that. The last one left me to die with you and I've never heard from him again."

There was no way Alexandra could ever tell her that to save her life he had to die. How could you tell your friend that? "It's strange that he has never called considering what a pain in the ass he was for so long."

"Well, you know that having your ass kicked by Alexandra could make you wanna stay away. I'm just sorry I was too out of it to see that. Plus, it totally wasn't cool him getting me doped up. I quit that shit and don't ever want to do it again." Karen was taking the lead and Alexandra followed as music blared before them. A stone building beckoned from ahead. The outside looked just like any of the other buildings, but the door was painted red and there was a sign glowing for some type of beer that Alexandra did not recognize.

"I can smell food." Alexandra was suddenly even hungrier. she opened the door and Karen walked in. She followed using her cane and making it look like she was having problems.

The bar was filled with a variety of people. Young and old, men and women, they all looked up for just a moment then went back to what they were doing. The bartender, an old man wearing a white shirt covered in the goo of the day, nodded at Karen. It was obvious this wasn't Karen's first time in the bar. They sat at the bar at two open chairs and Alexandra, after getting situated, hung her cane from the bar so she could reach it. Karen said a few words to the bartender, and he handed Alexandra a menu. The menu was in both English and Italian and it made it very easy for Alexandra to find a ravioli style dinner. Karen said a few words to the bartender, and he nodded handed them two beers and walked away to the kitchen.

"I see your Italian is getting better," Alexandra was impressed.

"Do you think you could do it as well?" Karen was curious.

"Maybe. I understood all of what you said but I'm not sure I could still say it as well. I wasn't the best at Italian. My recent interests have given me a lot of insight into Latin though."

"Yeah, we're in Rome, but they're dead. Not gonna get you very much here."

"You would be surprised." Alexandra took a drink of her beer. "Latin gives you an advantage in quite a lot."

"I think you just took it to show off. You always did think you were smarter than everybody. Well, you were smarter than everybody, but you didn't have to think you were smarter than everybody." Karen gulped down her beer in a single chug. "But you never could do that could you?"

"I'm not sure I ever would have wanted to." Alexandra took another sip of her beer and set it down smiling.

Karen scanned the bar and restaurant and her eyes lit up for a moment. "Wait here, I'll be right back."

Karen walked over to a table with an old man eating all alone. She began talking and pointing back and forth at Alexandra. After a moment, Karen walked back over and grabbed Alexandra and pointed down at her beer to the bartender who was returning. Alexandra grabbed her cane and walked over with Karen to the table. Karen sat down right away and pointed to another seat for Alexandra. As Alexandra sat down, Karen began talking.

"Alexandra this is Milos, he owns the bookstore here in town. It has been in his family for nine generations, and he is who you will get to talk to tomorrow."

Alexandra reached out her hand and the old man took it and put his hand over hers and shook it for just a moment. "It is good to meet you. Karen has said much about who you are and your interests in the old texts."

"I am sure she was too kind." Alexandra was speaking slowly knowing that English was a second language. "I appreciate you allowing me to look through all of the books you have collected."

"It will be fantastic," Milos seemed very happy; "no one has ever taken an interest in the volumes that young Karen has looked at. My father had collected those and his father before him had as well. I think you will find they are very complete."

The bartender brought another beer and a plate full of piping hot raviolis covered in mushrooms for Alexandra.

"I will be very interested. I do not have a lot of money and the cost to get here was expensive but if these are true, I am sure we will make a deal."

Milos smiled a big smile that showed his age. His teeth were worn and discolored but it was obvious that he was still full of life and excited about having Alexandra visit. "It will not matter if we make a deal. I would love to share with you the stories of the seven my father told me. There is so much to share, and I have papers and old maps, and many things that may excite you. Of course, it will be nice to have a beautiful young woman with me again. My poor wife died 15 years ago and left me alone. It would be nice to just talk to a woman. I appreciate you being so interested in the books about the seven."

"It will be good to talk to you," Alexandra smiled at the man; "I have found very little in the world and would like to do a paper about the legends."

Milos frowned. "It is likely those who procured the seven are keeping this knowledge hidden. My father told me that years ago he was offered a large amount of money to destroy the books. He refused and a fire started. The arsonist did not know that my father did not leave the books at the store. Instead, he kept them in his personal library. This curiosity pushed him to find more, and he searched all of Europe, as he could, and found copy after copy, including seven scrolls that define the seven original swords. The scrolls are written in an ancient cuneiform. My father attempted to translate them thinking they were Egyptian, but it is likely they are Sumerian or an earlier civilization yet to be discovered. The scrolls themselves are a miracle. They have never been copied and hold their ink and their form. My father would get them out from time to time and look at them because not only do they have the cuneiform, but they also have pictures of the seven with dimensions, and it could be their unique properties."

"That is most certainly fascinating." Alexandra found herself intrigued. "I look forward to reviewing them with you. I have managed to understand at least seven of the old cuneiform representations. It is my hope I will be able to translate or at least learn. Have you ever photographed the scrolls or the books?"

"No," Milos shook his head. "My father was always concerned that if someone found out they still existed, that we would be in danger. I only put them out last week as the store was in need of money. I am hopeful that with your help we can at least stay open another few months."

Alexandra winced. She didn't have enough money to keep a store in business, but she wasn't exactly sure what was going to be necessary. She continued eating and was overwhelmed by the flavor of the ravioli dish. "This is really good food."

Milos smiled. "This is my cousin's restaurant. I will let him know you are pleased."

"I am very pleased," Alexandra said as she finished her bowl; "Tell him the cook is amazing."

Milos laughed. "Of course, I will do so because he is the cook."

All three of them began laughing. The bartender came over, cleared the table, and brought another beer for Karen. Milos stood and nodded to the bartender. He tipped his head towards Alexandra. "I look forward to seeing you in the morning." Alexandra smiled and took another sip of her beer.

After Milos left Alexandra looked at Karen. "Why are we drinking beer in Italy?"

"Because I get drunk on wine too fast," Karen clicked her beer up in the air, and the two finished and paid. The walk back to the Airbnb was quick. Karen and Alexandra went in and sat down at the front table. Karen went to the refrigerator and got two more beers and brought them back. Alexandra laughed, and they drank the beers and went to bed.

Morning came fast, and Alexandra was up early. The shower was not as impressive as her own, but it felt good after the long plane ride. It's funny how being on a plane that varies from hot to cold constantly always makes you feel like you've been sweating for a day. Alexandra left her clothes but took her laptop, phone, and the series of notepads she had been creating over the last months. She was hoping this would give her some clue into the origins of her sword. After her conflict with Marjorie, Alexandra had been very concerned about what else may be lurking in the world. She realized after that short interaction that her discovery had put her in the crosshairs of a very old conflict.

Karen walked out into the living area and saw Alexandra dressed. "Let me get dressed, I'll go with you."

"You don't have to," Alexandra said; "I know you have a lot to do on your own."

"Don't be silly," Karen said; "I can be there for you."

"Why don't you stop by a little bit later and we'll get some lunch." Alexandra was opening the door; "it's not like the city is big enough to matter. You can find me pretty easy."

"I'll meet up with my class and then come find you. I suppose you know where the bookstore is?" Karen fiddled as she waited for an answer.

"I looked it up on Google and I'm heading right there. Not even a coffee in between."

"Okay, I'll see you there in an hour or two," Karen shuffled back to the bathroom as Alexandra closed the door.

The town was not very large and the walk to the bookstore was very easy. As Alexandra walked into the bookstore, she felt like she had fallen into a dream. Hardcover books were stacked to the ceiling on top of wooden bookshelves that were filled with books. It seemed that the entire store was a labyrinth of book after book, and although some bore familiar newer names, mixed in were hundreds that were dozens upon dozens of years old. Alexandra picked up a particularly old leather-bound book and opened it to see a press date of 1812. The book, "A History of Epidemic Cholera," was worn, but readable. She looked at the book for a moment, then put it back on the pile. She surmised it was worth money, but she was not looking for rare finds to build her library.

Milos stepped out from behind a pile of books several rows back. He was wearing older black pants a dress shirt with an open vest hanging over the shirt. His thin glasses were on the tip of his nose, and he was looking at a volume in his hand with three other books in his other hand. He closed the book and put it on a shelf and began moving another direction until he saw Alexandra.

"Oh, I see you're here early," Milos set the books on a shelf and walked down the aisle towards her with his hand outstretched. "It is good to see you, so very good. I trust you slept well. I have set up a small table for you in the back. There you can decide what books are the ones you are looking for. I'm sure you will find many. I have tried to keep them well organized but as you can see, I tend to find a great many books. There are also two other buildings behind this one full of reading material. Do you think reading has been forgotten? I see so many children from America and other countries reading or playing on their electronic devices and so few carrying books. It saddens me to think that books may be gone."

"I think there will always be people who rise above and continue to read. The rest will fall away as time passes."

"That is a unique statement from one so young. Karen tells me that you have a terminal disease. She says right now it is in remission but the disease itself is incurable."

Alexandra looked down at her cane. "That is correct, the disease is incurable. It is a rare form of muscular dystrophy and explaining it always makes people's eyes glaze over. Eventually my muscles will deteriorate to a point that I will die."

"For one so young, that is difficult. Come with me and let me show you to what you were looking for."

Alexandra and Milos walked to the back where a small table was set up with one rickety wooden chair. To the side of the table was a bookshelf filled with very old hardcover leather-bound books. On the table was a book that had an etching in the front that matched her sword, the sword of Fury, and on the back of the cover was the puzzle that her sword was encased in.

"Please look around the store as you see fit. My store is yours. I will be working on new books and putting them away. I may be able to answer questions if you have them. My father could answer more but he refused to come down."

"Your father, he is still alive?" Alexandra asked.

"Yes, he is alive and well. He keeps to himself now and tends to make wine and make love to his young wife."

"That must be awesome." Alexandra could not believe Milos' father was still alive. She shook her head and sat down at the table with her backpack and her cane.

Milos wandered off, then picked up the books he had set down earlier. Alexandra opened the book on the table and began reading what she could understand. The book turned out to be partially written in Egyptian and partially in Sumerian. Alexandra spent a significant amount of effort trying to translate one page at a time. She was not sure what the book was penned in, but the actual ink had not been recopied and was relatively faded. After the first few pages, she found the picture of her sword and worked on translating the transcription beneath it. The wording was fairly difficult, but she was able to surmise that the sword of Fury was the seventh of the seven swords. The translation noted that the wielder of the sword of Fury could find peace, fire, or fury if they held the sword and felt the world through its blade. Alexandra worked on that passage for a short time and still, could not come up with a translation she could understand. How can you feel the world through the blade of the sword?

She stopped on those cuneiforms and worked forward. There were numerous passages about other swords, but she was not seeing the right words to go with the meanings. Each time she thought she had it, the words eluded her, and she became increasingly frustrated.

Then she realized that one of the symbols she had been translating as *man* was actually *mankind* and that the distinction between men and women was not made inside of the book. She also realized that the cuneiforms were not any hieroglyph that she had worked with before. She wondered how it had actually got into a book and how someone would have a working history of the seven swords that was far older.

Still, some just didn't fit. She tried different combinations of words until there was a tap on her shoulder that made her turn fast and jump up.

"Easy," Karen stepped back; "I just thought we could get some lunch together."

"What time is it?" Alexandra had no idea.

"It's 1:00 PM Italy time, you've been here for quite a while now." Karen glanced at the books that Alexandra was studying. "Yuck, and I thought calculus sucked. This looks a lot worse."

"It's actually pretty interesting, at least what I can discern so far." Alexandra was smiling as she spoke; "there's a lot of history that I have never heard of before. This isn't about the sword or the swords but about the battles surrounding them. It has information about the sword I have but not much so far about the others. They are mentioned." Alexandra grabbed a pad and flipped through it for a moment. "They are mentioned as the six brethren of mankind. It seems that each of the swords represent a key element of humankind and each of the swords has similar and unique properties. They are all named as well."

Karen was obviously bored already. "Would you like to go find a nice sandwich? There's a deli here that makes killer subs. Better than any subway I know of."

"Let me clean up. I don't want to be a burden. I've been taking pictures of the different books, so I have a backup, but these are fascinating."

"Have you talked to Milos about price?" Karen was a little curious.

"No, not yet; I've seen him out of the corner of my eye, but he's been busy, and I've left him alone."

"Let's go find him before we leave," Karen was very diligent. She always wanted to make sure that she was doing for others.

They walked up and down the aisles and the bookstore was much larger than Alexandra expected. There were significant rows in the front but as they went farther back, they widened out, and as Milos had said, there were a number of other buildings interconnected. Normally Alexandra would be geeked out at all the books and paying close attention. Now, she was focused on the history of the seven swords. They finally found Milos in the back. "We were going to go get some lunch, would you like to go as well?"

"That would be nice, why don't we walk up to my father's villa and speak to him. I have lunch with him every day and there is always plenty."

"We don't want to impose," Alexandra looked at Karen; "but I would love to meet your father and know about some of the books I have been looking at. Do you know if he translated any of them?"

"I'm sure he would love to talk to you. Let's go visit with him. His wife, Anna, will be so thrilled to have company. I will ring them and let them know we are walking up." Milos walked over to the phone and dialed the number on the old rotary set. He spoke rapidly in Italian smiling and laughing the entire time. "Come, come. It is fine, they would be excited to have visitors."

Karen and Alexandra looked at each other, then nodded and followed Milos out the door. The day turned out to be quite beautiful and a cool breeze was blowing across the small village. They walked up the street and turned, walking up a hill. The road became bracketed by long tall grass on one side and strung grapes on the other. As they walked up the light incline Alexandra was happy that she no longer really needed her cane. Not too long ago, she would not have been able to climb this hill. Not too long ago, she would have needed a wheelchair or a car ride.

As they walked up the hill a beautiful Tuscan home came into view. It was two stories high and probably at least 10,000 square feet set into a wide shape with a courtyard in the center sporting an ornate fountain. The asphalt turned to cobblestone as they came closer to the house and the precisely laid cobblestone went all the way up to the front door. As they approached the door it opened wide and the man who could have easily been Milos' brother stepped out and grabbed Milos tight. "It is always good to see you, my son." He looked to Karen and Alexandra, "My name is Nicholas. Who do we have here?"

Karen stepped forward first and put out her hand. "Hi I'm Karen, I'm here with the college from the United States. This is my roommate, Alexandra. When I saw some of the books you had in the bookstore, I called her, and she flew right over. She has a fascination with ancient languages and swords, and the volumes you have were exactly what she was looking for."

"Which books are you referring to?" Nicholas looked at Milos.

"The old volumes that you collected years ago. I was cleaning out the warehouse and I put them up in the antique book area." Milos moved towards the door as a beautiful woman came out. "Ladies, this is my stepmother, Anna."

Anna couldn't have been more than 40 and was as beautiful as any fashion model on a runway. Her long black hair was pulled back into a ponytail, but it looked crisp as though she had just done it. Her skin was olive-colored, and she wore a very fashionable pair of khaki slacks and a white silk blouse. Her nails were done, and it looked like her skin was near-perfect.

"It is a pleasure to meet you, girls. I have lunch ready for us in the garden." Anna opened the door wide to a beautiful hall. As the girls walked in front of the two men, they could see the open area that widened out to a back patio. They walked through the house and a table was already set with plates and silver covers over top of those plates.

"You didn't have to go to any trouble." Alexandra felt like she was in a mansion.

"No, no, it is no trouble," Anna said in broken English; "We rarely get visitors, and it is so nice to have someone from America visit. I do not get to practice my English as often as I should."

"Thank you for your hospitality," Karen said.

The two men were not around. They showed up a few minutes later and Milos was a bit sad. Alexandra was not sure what had bothered him, and Karen didn't immediately notice. They all sat down at the table and Anna stood back up and took the covers off of the food. Neatly sliced sandwiches and fruit we're on the plates, and it looked as though each item was placed with mathematical precision.

"This looks beautiful," Karen took a picture with her phone. "I can't believe how lovely this is. I feel like I'm in a movie."

It was quiet at first as they began eating but Alexandra broke the silence. "Nicholas, I hope you don't mind my asking, but I was having some problems with the translation of some of the cuneiforms in the books your son says you collected. Do you know what period they are from?"

Nicholas wiped his mouth and glanced at his son before looking back at Alexandra. "I don't know what I should say. There has been a mistake. My son invertedly put those books out to try to gain money. He could have just asked for money, but he is ashamed. The books are from my personal collection and were not meant to be seen by others. They are quite priceless, and I doubt anyone could afford what I would need in order to sell them. I am glad that you got some work done with him, but I apologize; they will not be leaving with you."

"I am so sorry Alexandra," Milos bowed his head; "I did not mean for you to come this far and leave empty handed."

"Can we at least discuss the books for a moment even if I can't take them?"

"I don't think that's going to be possible," Nicholas said. "The cuneiform in the books is very old and I doubt anyone would be able to translate it."

"I am very close to translating the book that is important to me. I was having some problems with some symbols regarding the seven. I was hoping you could help me. I am willing to pay just for some knowledge."

Milos looked over at his father with a hopeful eye.

Nicholas took a sip of wine. "Why is this so important to you?"

"It is of a personal nature," Alexandra replied.

"I'm afraid," Nicholas began, "I'm sorry; Alexandra could you join me in my study for a moment."

"Yes, Sir I can," Alexandra replied as she stood. She walked with her cane and began to follow Nicholas. It didn't take them very long to walk inside and to the left into an ornate library. Nicholas closed the door behind them.

"I need to know why you are so interested in the volumes."

"Curiosity I suppose."

"If you lie to me again, I will kill you."

Alexandra tensed immediately. "You wouldn't believe me if I told you."

"I'm afraid I must insist. Your answer will determine the fate of you and your friend."

Alexandra took a deep breath. She looked at the man before her who had no real age. He was one of the gentlemen that could have been from anytime. He was wearing white slacks and a yellow short sleeve shirt with deep tan arms that were well-muscled. She looked at him and was unsure of how to answer. In the end, she decided the truth was best. "I found the box months ago with a puzzle on it. I bought it as a decoration. As I cleaned it, I have figured out what the puzzle was and how to solve it. When I solved it, it gave me access to a sword. The sword has special properties and has already caused me issue with a psychotic librarian. I am trying to find the origin of the sword and who else I may have to face because of my discovery."

Nicholas pondered for a moment and looked out the window to Karen, Anna, and his son. "Who else knows you have come here?"

"No one." She was being honest and probably too confident in her abilities if there was trouble, "Karen called me, and I flew over. I told no one the reason."

Nicholas looked down, turned around, and looked at his desk. "I suppose I couldn't keep it hidden forever but I have tried. Why do you want to know about the sword?"

"It has unique properties, and I would like to know where they came from." Alexandra realized that Nicholas was now more than he seemed.

"And those properties are?"

"Before I answer, can you tell me what's going on? I'm answering questions and you are giving me nothing. Not exactly fair." Alexandra tensed a little waiting for a response.

"Alexandra, are you a good person or a bad person?"

"I'm trying to figure that out. I'm not sure what other people

143

would say any more. Because of the disease I had, I was bitter and angry with the world. Now I feel like I have something to live for, and I saved my friend's life. It was something I never would have thought of doing in the past but now it seems almost like second nature. I feel like there's something more important than this world. I feel like my responsibilities are larger now."

"That is the American in you talking," Nicholas chuckled; "I once believed the same. How many people have you met that have asked you about the sword?"

"Just the librarian. She told me that she had destroyed most of the documentation about the seven. At the time, she thought she was going to kill me, so I don't think she originally meant to say it."

"What is this woman calling herself now?"

"She called herself Marjorie, she was a librarian at our school." Alexandra was trying desperately to connect the dots. "Do you know her?"

"Probably," Nicholas said. "She's only had a sword for a few hundred years. Because of that, she is still trying to control everything. I am not so concerned. I am not certain why I'm going to trust you, but I will tell you that I have been harboring this secret for hundreds of years. Perhaps even thousands. You see, the swords have unique properties as you have stated, but you probably have only experienced a small part of those. I am not certain if you were meant to have the sword, but in my experience the sword will not show itself except to someone who is able to wield it. The problem is that the sword can be wielded by either a good or evil person. This is why I asked you if you were a good person. Your librarian is not a good person. I am aware that she has tried to take the swords from other guardians. It is quite difficult to understand her motivation. What I know now is that for the first time in an exceptionally long time, I will have to move on just in case she now knows where I am. Either that, or I will have to face her. I have lost contact with the other bearers over the years. Each is a guardian of the sword, and the sword is a guardian of the man. I am not sure which sword you have but someone had to die for you to be able to wield the sword. I assume your disease is now gone?"

"Yes, it is now gone," Alexandra was fascinated.

"And did you have to kill for that disease to be gone?" Nicholas asked.

"Yes, it was an accident at first, but the second person had killed Karen. She was going to die, and I used the sword to save her in the process."

"I am not sure how your balance will be then. The sword is like a scale. All seven are. If you use them for evil, they will help you become more evil. If you use them for good, they will help you become better. There is one who may remain neutral by doing both good and evil, but this is a tough road to take as well. What is your intention with the sword?"

"My intention?" Alexandra was confused.

"Do you intend to be a good person and use the sword for justice, or do you intend to be a bad person and use the sword for yourself?"

"I haven't really thought about it yet. If I see inside myself, I have only used it for justice so far. I know this justice is brutal with the first men, but my intention was not to be brutal. My intention was to save myself and then my friend. I haven't considered much more as I didn't know the source of the sword's power and did not want to use it if it was negative."

"A wise choice young lady." Nicholas looked back out at his wife and son. "I will help you learn. I am the one who wrote the notes you were trying to translate. I can help you learn as long as you stay positive. I will also then be able to keep an eye on you to make certain you are going in the right direction."

Alexandra was dumbfounded. "If you wrote those books, they are hundreds of years old."

"Actually, they are thousands of years old. Anna is my 16th wife. I have had many sons and daughters and eventually, I will disappear and start a new life. For now, I will see if I can change the flow of information and avoid running into problems with your Marjorie. I am hopeful that with positive reinforcement you can eventually become a guardian as we all have."

"I'm not sure what I want," Alexandra stammered; "this is an awful lot to take in."

"You don't seem to understand that it wasn't just you who chose the sword. It was the sword who chose you. It is a two-way street, and depending upon which sword you have, they can be quite finicky. When they were forged, it was to keep humanity from destroying themselves. Unfortunately, over thousands of years, the shift between good and evil is constantly in motion. This is why I asked if you were a good person. If you were a bad person, I would have already killed you."

Alexandra stepped back unconsciously. "Killed me?"

"You have to understand this is bigger than you and your friend. The ownership of the swords controls the world. It may not seem like something so small can make such a big difference but if evil controls the swords, the world will lean towards evil. When they were forged, all seven were with good men and women, but the reason there are seven is there will never be a perfect balance. The world will ever be leaning towards good or towards evil based on the 7th sword. In the history of the swords, it has never been as it is today, and I suspect that there are four evil swords now. It's not that they do evil or that they are looking for anything in particular, it is just that the balance seems shifted. It is partially my fault, as I love my young Anna and have not tried to find any of the bearers. Perhaps now it is time."

Again, Alexandra was stunned. "What you are saying is if I am a good person the world will shift towards good, and if I am a bad person the world will shift towards bad? I'm not sure how to tell you this but nobody agrees on what good or bad is anymore, and I'm not sure who I believe in as far as politics right now."

"I know this is a lot to take in, let's finish lunch and walk to the bookstore." Nicholas walked out of the library as Alexandra looked out into the garden again. The table was empty.

Alexandra turned as Nicholas ducked and a blade cut through the door and the wall next to him. The blade came loose and pulled back as Marjorie stepped into view. Alexandra looked at the woman and at Nicholas.

"It's good to see you again Vladimir, or is it Nicholas now?" Marjorie grinned with an evil malevolence.

"I would have been happy never seeing you again. Still trying to erase history and disappear into the background?"

"Of course, I am." Marjorie held her sword forward as she entered the room. "This world would not accept things as they are. They explain it away and it is hard to dodge missiles and bullets. Better to live in stealth and shape the world by words."

"You're still a dreamer who thinks they can change the world as they see fit. We are only guides; we are not meant to decide how the world will be."

"Tell that to those I have vanquished. This child has the sword of Fury because its owner hid its location to keep it from me. They have all become more cautious. When I have two swords all of you will fall."

"If you've read anything that was written, you know that's not how it works. If you have two swords, you will die."

"You know that is not true. The text is inconclusive. It is just that no one person has ever had the resolve to wield two swords. I have that resolve," Marjorie smirked. "And I have two possibilities here to take a second sword."

"You know you will not take it from me." Nicholas took a step in front of Alexandra. "And I will not let you take it from her. You should have chosen an easier target."

"Oh, the mighty Vladimir or Nicholas or Arthur. You who think that you are above all others. Haven't you figured it out? Even with the swords there are ways to kill us all. None of the seven are safe in this world of advanced weapons. Perhaps I should demonstrate that right now."

Marjorie moved out of the way and a man stepped to the end of the room with a strange looking rifle. Alexandra realized as she saw a spark that it was a flamethrower and not any type of conventional weapon. The flame grew and grew towards Alexandra. Nicholas reached out his hand and a magnificently tall sword was there. The quillons shone of brass or gold and the blade was long and thin. Marjorie smiled but Nicholas spun the sword, and the flames were redirected towards her. She was not fast enough to block them all and she screamed in pain. The attacker with the flamethrower continued his fire and Alexandra couldn't stand by and watch.

Alexandra reached out her hand, called to her sword, and it was there. She moved forward to the right of the flames and felt the heat singe her hair but that didn't stop her. She slid the sword straight down at the weapon trying to push it down but had never realized how sharp the sword was as it sliced steel, aluminum, and plastic without even a pause. The weapon fell forward and with the mechanism damaged, the flames began surrounding the man's hands. He let go of the trigger, but the flames were still there.

Nicholas stood up and looked much different as he moved forward towards Marjorie. He was almost noble and stoic. Marjorie's face was burned badly on the side, and it looked as though much of her arm and torso were blackened as well. She surveyed the situation through cloudy eyes and in a move no one expected, she plunged her sword into her own gunman. His body disappeared as well as the flamethrower, but the effect was near immediate as her face healed and her body showed through the charred remains of her clothing.

Nicolas stood as Marjorie ran out of the room. He walked out the door to follow and jumped back into the room as gunfire erupted. Shots were being fired constantly, likely from fully automatic weapons. Nicholas looked at Alexandra holding the sword of Fury.

"Do you know how to use the sword?" Nicolas looked at the walls and the windows heading out of the room.

"I'm pretty good with the sword but only as a sword," Alexandra stated; "as I was reading, it appears the sword has other properties that I have no idea how to master."

"That answers that question," Nicholas looked around. "Your sword has numerous properties well beyond that of a simple sword. I'm assuming you have used its healing properties but that was likely done by accident, right?"

Alexandra nodded.

"Well, it's time to learn," Nicholas said. "I want you to spin the pommel in your hand and just roll it back and forth like you were playing with a toy. Point it at the door and start walking towards the door."

Alexandra put the sword in her hands and pointed directly towards the ceiling and then began spinning the pommel. After the second spin there was a hum in the room and as she walked towards the door, she saw that bullets were being deflected to the far wall.

"You're going to have to trust me now. Walk it into the hallway and start walking towards the gunmen. I will take care of the rest. As long as you keep rolling the sword you will be fine."

Alexandra was a little concerned, but she continued walking

until she was in the hall facing the three gunmen. They were spraying bullets constantly at her with three machine guns and the bullets careened off whatever force the sword was creating. Nicholas was behind her and one of the gunmen fell, hit by a ricocheted bullet. The two other men ran out of ammo almost simultaneously and dropped their magazines as they fumbled to grab another. Nicholas was far faster. A single arched slice cut both men in half from his sword. As the two men began to fall, their bodies dissolved to ash as Alexandra had seen before with her own sword. The third man was rolling on the ground and Nicholas pressed his sword directly through him. He too was soon a pile of ashes.

"We need to find your friend and my family." Alexandra followed as Nicholas ran through the house. At the end of the hallway Marjorie held Milos. As she saw both Alexandra and Nicholas come around the corner she cursed and threw Milos to the floor. She started to swing her blade down upon him, but Alexandra had learned and started rolling her sword as she ran to Milos. Marjorie's blade hit an invisible barrier and stopped dead as Alexandra moved forward.

Marjorie pulled her sword back and stepped backwards cautiously. Then in an unexpected move, she swung wide through stone and wood splitting the frame of the door. The frame fell in upon itself and blocked their way. As the dust settled, they could hear Marjorie running and a car rapidly leaving the area.

"Thank you for my son's life," Nicholas was helping Milos up. Nicholas now looked like the son and Milos the father. Explanations would be necessary to his family. "We need to go. Now that she knows where we are we will not be safe here."

"I'm sorry," Alexandra noted. "I didn't think I was followed."

"It's probably my fault," Karen said. "I posted on Instagram a picture of the bookstore and one of the unique book covers."

Alexandra looked down at the ground. "I suppose it's my fault for trying to find how to use this sword properly and to understand its history."

"We will go to the bookstore, and I will give you the books for you to translate and eventually understand. I suggest you leave immediately. Get a flight back to the States and find a new place to live. It will be important that you learn more about your sword and all of the unique properties it has. It will be even more important that you stay safe and that you keep your friend and any family safe. I will find you when my family is safe and we will review the swords together."

"What if I want to stay where I am?" Alexandra asked.

"Then you will face Marjorie over and over. She will find a way to get you."

"And if I find a way to get her?" Alexandra was confident.

"Then make sure her sword gets to a good person because right now, based on the situation of the world, you and I maybe the only one's wielding positive swords."

"Do you really believe that the ownership of the swords guides the entire world?" Alexandra was skeptical.

"Of course, I do, and you will eventually as well. You will see it in time. It won't be something big. It will be subtle in how people treat each other. You will suddenly just know."

"I'll be watching," Alexandra said as they walked to the bookstore with Karen following closely behind.

"I'm sorry I messed up," Karen said; "but can you tell me what just happened? Should I stay here with my class or go?"

"We've got a lot to talk about," Alexandra replied. "Let's get home and we'll work it out. Your class will wait, and they will understand if you tell them I needed you. Thanks for being my friend, my best friend."

They Walk Among Us

I stumbled into the well-lit bar and looked up at the lights. Only seconds ago, I saw them in my mind as candles floating in a chandelier of steel and crystal. Above me now was the same ornate fixture holding bright LED lights. The bar was called the Elusive Lounge and was on my list of places to check out.

A petite young woman walked up to me, "We'll be closing soon. Would you like to sit at the bar, or would you like a table?"

I stuttered in my mind, and I am sure I looked like a confusing mess, "What is this building?"

"You are at the Elusive," she announced; "Do you need me to call someone for you? Are you okay?"

"I'm fine," I replied, struggling a little with the overwhelming sensations assailing my psyche. "Can I have a small table?"

"Of course," she responded as she picked up a menu and walked towards a second open area in the quaint establishment. The young woman walked me to a four-spot table and set the menu on top, along with some silverware. "My name is Rachel," she said as she turned; "Spelled the right way and easy to pronounce. We close in 35 minutes. The kitchen will cook up to then, so don't worry. What would you like to drink?"

My mind was clearing, and I could see the present far more easily now, so I smiled. "Hi Rachel, I'm Dan. How about a bourbon and a water, please?"

"I will be right back with that," Rachel replied.

I scanned the room and saw it as it was today, not as the amalgam of memories of yesteryear I saw minutes ago. I was back in the now, and it felt far better than the jumbled mess I had felt only moments ago. I was sure the bourbon would not help that much. Alcohol only made it worse.

Rachel came back with my drink and set it on the table. I saw her more clearly now. She appeared to be in her early twenties with chestnut brown hair pulled into a tight ponytail. She could easily be ready for a hike or a run as much as working here. Despite the late hours, she appeared fresh and prepared to take on the world with near-perfect makeup and no hair out of place. That in itself was suspicious. When I worked bar, I was covered in muck all the time, smelled like the bar, and had hair that looked like I had a livewire installed in my anus. "Anything to snack on or eat?"

I nodded, "Pick something for me."

"Okay, what do you like?" Rachel asked.

"I like everything, pick your favorite," I said and saw her searching for the correct answer. "How about the Cajun Fritters?"

She laughed and was at ease again, "Good choice." As she turned to leave, I noticed her ponytail swing from side to side like the pendulum of a clock. Time, I seemed to have time, but there was never enough.

"Rachel?" I had to go ahead and see why I was here.

She turned and looked at me with an inquisitive look, likely born out of the many that heard her name but never repeated it. "Yes?"

"Is this building haunted?" I watched her reaction.

It appeared as though a chill sizzled through her spine, and she feigned a smile for a second. "What?"

"I mean, do you know the history of this building or if it has ever been haunted?" I asked again.

"Well," Rachel took a deep breath and looked around the mostly empty area I was seated in as if struggling to find words. "The owner says it is haunted and teases about it, and we all know there are things that are a bit weird. Strange things that happen at night, and ever weirder things that we find sometimes." She glanced up at the large television hanging above us. "Take that TV. We cleaned it and got up on a ladder because of all the fingerprints. No one could reach the TV, and when Michelle and I looked at the back of it, there were huge handprints with long fingers. They couldn't have been anyone from here. It was just creepy."

I looked at the TV, and my vision shifted for a minute. The 14-foot tall specter was standing in front of the TV and grabbed it and tried to wrench it from the ceiling. The TV did not move, and the specter wailed in agony. Long white hair flowed from its head, and though the thin wispy body was misshapen, it was obviously a woman wearing a floor-length white gown. They reached up again and grabbed at the television, only to scream again.

"We also have had issues with the basement," Rachel continued, breaking my concentration from the frightful specter.

"The basement?" I asked as my vision cleared, and I again focused on this young woman.

"Yeah," Rachel began; "The owner said someone died down there or was killed there by a murderer. I have never tried to look it up. A few years ago, someone broke in after taking some mushrooms. They somehow made it to the basement and threw up everywhere. I am talking piles of nasty green stuff. When we found them, they were shivering and muttering something about not letting him take them."

"Sounds like fun," I replied, wondering how bad the basement could be. "Sorry, I am taking your time."

"No, I like being scared, but this place creeps me out. I have been in the basement and felt like someone was watching me; it just feels weird. I have never been afraid of anything, but I won't go down there at night. It just seems more alive and wanting something."

"You've never seen anything yourself, though?" I pressed.

"No," Rachel was cautious now, and her eyes drifted, "I mean, I believe in that stuff, but I wouldn't think it would ever happen to me. I mean, I don't get scared, and nothing in this place is gonna take me or really bother me at all."

"Brave, huh?" I asked with a slight grin.

"Oh crap," Rachel jumped and moved away, "I need to order your fritters before they close the kitchen."

Rachel scurried away, and I watched her with fascination. I stood and walked the rooms of the small bar and grill. It was much larger than I had envisioned in my psychic-induced stupor. I saw it differently when I walked in. It was not massive or small. I suppose it was just right. There was a built-up game room with a ping-pong table and a few paintings on the wall. In one of the paintings, I saw a tree with a swing. The swing was empty along a purple horizon while someone stood in the grass. My mind drifted, and a voice echoed, "The little girl is still there." The swing began moving back and forth. A figure appeared and disappeared in the swing, and the figure in the field moved. All at once, the swing was empty again. "The little girl is still there," I heard again as my vision returned to normal.

Trying to keep my composure, I returned to my table and sat down. This gift, or curse, had been mine for my whole life. When I was younger, I had never known when I would see or not see, but as

I hit my thirties, it jumped into overdrive. A bit of strangeness and my mind would drift between times and between the normal and paranormal worlds like some fantastical cartoon. I remember seeing "ParaNorman" and wondering how many others possessed this curse as it described how I saw things far more accurately than I could ever relay. I also thought of the series "Odd Thomas" by Dean Koontz and wondered if he, too, saw the things that went bump in the night or if he had an active imagination filled with my daily excitement and over-the-top nightmares. I could not be the only one.

I had only told three people since I discovered how I actually saw the world. My Grandmother, who told me it was in our family for years, and a friend and his grandfather when I was staying on an Indian reservation. My friend was talking about the Spirit world. When I told him about what I saw, he took me to his grandfather, and they told me I was chosen. To this day, they never have told me what I was chosen for, but I often wished it was the lottery instead of semi-hot girls in lingerie that have been dead for far too long.

I moved my chair to see the paintings as I waited for Rachel and my food to return. I blurred my vision and watched the swing move back and forth. I heard the voice again, "The little girl is here," and a giggle this time. I shook my head and was back as Rachel walked up.

Looking around, I watched the last couple leave, leaving me alone in the building with the staff. Rachel set the fritters down as well as the water and bourbon. "Take your time. We will be here for a while."

"Rachel," I asked before she turned; "is there anything else about this place that is weird?"

"Not really," Rachel fidgeted as she spoke. "I mean, the owner bought it to keep it as it was. The place pays for itself, and we make good money working here. It is a good life." I smiled, tasted the fritter, and watched as Rachel considered, "You sure are interested. Any reason why?"

"No," I was deciding how to word my reply. "Not really. I was just out walking, and this place pretty much drew me in." It wasn't really a lie, and that felt good for once.

Rachel laughed but eyed me slightly as she said, "I will be back."

As she walked away, I looked again at the television, and my eyes blurred again. The figure in the long nightdress was again looking at the television, watching the empty screen. Again, she reached up to the silent TV and tried to move it, then shrieked in silence. I looked around and saw no one else. "I can turn that on for you, if you like."

The figure turned to me. The long hair and long dress were fitted around a misshapen, overly thin body. The hair and complexion reminded me of the movie "The Ring" and the ghastly pallor of Samara. I smiled and kept my cool. Usually, the spirits I could see could not hurt me. Well, for the most part, I considered as I glanced at a scar on the back of my hand. She looked at me and moved, and my eyes followed her. She seemed curious and came forward; though she was not truly there, I could almost smell the fetid scent of death coming from her spectral breath. Her sunken eyes regarded me. She seemed like she would speak as Rachel returned and handed me the check.

"Who were you talking to?" she asked.

"Um, no one," I replied.

"I heard you," Rachel was focused on me. "You were talking to her."

"Who?" I asked, "No one is here."

157

Rachel closed her eyes and then sat down across from me. "What are we going to do with you?"

"Umm, do with me?" I asked and looked around for the "We."

The door to the kitchen swung open, and two other girls and three men walked out and came to my table. As Rachel sat, the other five stepped around me, forming a small circle.

"He sees her," Rachel barked without taking her eyes from me.

I stood and leaned against the wall, "No, I don't see anyone."

"You can still see me," Rachel was nonchalant. "You shouldn't be able to see me now."

I cleared my head, and Rachel faded in and out, "What the…" I began.

"Sit down," the older man was calm as he spoke. "We need to talk."

I sat back down at my table cautiously and listened.

"How can you see us?" he asked.

"I don't know," I was honest as I told them; "it is something I have always been able to see a little more than everyone else. It is just worse now. What is going on?"

"Why are you here?" he asked.

"I was drawn here," I acknowledged as I considered why in the back of my mind. "I am not sure why. It just happens."

They turned to each other and talked. The discussion was fast, and I could barely understand.

The older man turned to me. "I am Claude. This is our place. We recently made it ours after suffering through plenty of problems with owner after owner being pretty horrible. Day after day, we would see people mistreated and our home degraded to nothing. We can leave, but it is a comfort to stay in one place, and this was ours. One day Rachel found she could shift to a tangible form. On that day, she applied here, where she lived, and began working for the owner. With practice and patience, we all eventually could shift to the real world for a while and did. Each of us taking a job and being praised for being such good workers. It was easy to convince each owner to let us work for cash, and we stayed off the radar. Over time, we saved money and finally bought this building through the miracles of the Internet."

"How could you do that without ID and a bank account?" I asked, curious as I paid attention to the group looking for an opening to leave. How can you outrun a ghost anyway?

"You would be surprised what can be done with the Internet," Claude was open as he spoke. "The Internet has truly opened an avenue for us to be more, to have what seems like life for the dead. I know most spirits have no such ability. Some drift in and out, and we watch them while the normal patrons are completely oblivious. After all, who would ever consider we could all be solid spectral beings? We can't be sure what has given us this gift, but we can use it and do our best. We make careful decisions and do everything we can to be unnoticed. Now we have to decide what to do with you?"

"With me?" I asked.

"You are a risk to us," Claude smiled. "Not a big risk as you would be called a crackpot if you went out screaming this to anyone or the press, but someone might believe you, and we can't have that, can we? We have slowly taken time to cleanse the Internet of past hauntings here, and Rachel has become quite adept at using

159

computers and systems.”

“What about her?” I pointed to the television, and the lithe ghost now watching me instead of the television.

“She will do as I say,” Claude noted. “She is not strong enough to be here with us. Her presence is more of an annoyance than any assistance.”

I took a bite of the fritter. “I have to say, for a dead guy, you make good food.”

“I would say thank you, but I think there is a big ‘but’ in your words,” Claude replied.

“Just kill him,” Rachel declared.

“There is a big butt, and I cannot lie,” I stalled. “If you kill me, I can’t leave a good review.”

One of the other men moved forward a little. “He is trying to distract us in hopes we are not bound well.”

“I don’t think you are too tightly wrapped if that’s what you’re saying,” I laughed, watching and blurring from here to there. “I just want to know what’s in the basement?” My humor seemed to be unexpected, and that was good.

They all stopped and looked side to side. Somewhere, I had struck a nerve. Rachel’s statement was not a lie. Something about the basement was different. As I blurred in and out, I saw the lithe spirit nod to me and point to the slightly open door to the basement. Her grisly appearance shifted; somewhere in the shifting, I saw a beautiful young woman, but it was gone again.

“There’s nothing in the basement,” Rachel uttered in a near-nervous tone. How do ghosts get nervous anyway?

I looked at my untouched bourbon and picked it up. With my right hand, I reached into my pocket and found the near-ancient stick lighter I had used for a dozen years. I took a drink and sprayed the bourbon in the air as I lit the lighter. The resulting fireball should have taken my face off. I was lucky. The fireball was bright and did not burn me. It did allow me to jump up and run to the basement door. I rushed down the stairs.

"Get him," I heard behind me, but there was no shuffling, diving, or pouncing on me. As I reached the basement floor, nausea flowed over me. My mind shifted, and I saw the years fall away before my eyes. As I did, I saw a man look over at me. He was massive and there and not there all at once. He looked at me and then to the stairs where two pseudo spirits had rushed down in my pursuit. It was hard to concentrate. There was so much going on in the present and in whatever hellish time I was seeing that I was not sure what was happening. The monstrous spirit must have been in my time, not just a vision, as he grabbed the first pursuer and pulled them to him. A scream echoed in and out of my mind, and I was unsure if sound or soul made my head resonate. The shriek intensified and became a wail of utter despair. My mind felt as though it would explode with the sensation. I looked around in my clouded vision and saw the stairwell at the back of the basement leading up to the street or alley. I didn't care where it went as long as it was away from here.

I turned and saw the vast monstrosity's jaw unhinge as though it were an enormous snake of some kind as it slowly devoured the spirit from upstairs. The maw was colossal, and the male spirit who had spoken before was shoved inch by inch into the mouth of his attacker. As I watched, I noticed a beautiful young woman smile at me and then change back to the tall spirit who guided me here. She drifted up the stairs in an almost satisfied manner as the second pursuer rushed to safety above. I ran to the basement alley stairs and pushed to the top.

As I climbed, each step seemed covered in molasses, but I made it to the rusted doorway. I turned to see the hulking spirit heading towards me, apparently not satiated by his ectoplasmic hors d'oeuvre. He was in no hurry, but my frantic push at the door became more energetic as the latch finally opened, and I emerged into a dark alleyway. I slammed the rust-covered door behind me, stumbled down the alley, and found my way to the street. As I walked past the front of the bar, I saw Rachel glaring at me with a frustrated look. She faded in and out while behind her, I saw the spirit who had somehow saved me. In her grisly countenance, I saw a smile. Her nightgown flowed around her as though she were in the wind; for an instant, I saw her as a beautiful woman.

My nausea faded as I saw the lights go off in the bar behind me. So many questions raced through my mind. Who was in the basement, and who was the trapped spirit? I shuddered though at the thought of the ghost the monstrosity caught. What was it like to die if you were already dead? I trembled at the thought and walked as far as I could from this place. At least for now.

Free Gift

My name is Tim. I'm not anyone really special, I'm just another person in the crowd. I never realized how true that was until recently. I was going to work as usual, and as I walked down the busy streets of New York City, I passed a long series of tables advertising free headphones. Usually, tables like this are a scam, and I walk by without giving it a second glance. The vendors who are trying to get you to walk up give you a song and dance, and by the time you walk away, the free item has become free plus half the money you have and maybe a little extra. This was a little different. The table was filled with small boxes and as people walked by, they glanced at the items, as I was, and then picked up a box putting them in their purse or their pocket and continued on their way. A few people grabbed two or three, but most people were honoring the sign that said, "please just take one."

I was intrigued because rarely, if ever, had I ever found something that didn't have a catch. After all, the stories of a free puppy were fairly true, and a free puppy is not something that is really free. I picked up one of the small boxes and put it in my satchel and made my way to the giant building downtown that housed my company.

As I walked in the door, I glanced to the east and saw another table full of headphones. Like the previous table, people were walking by and picking up items almost as fast as two men could stock them. Whoever was giving away all of these wireless earbuds was spending a lot of money to get market penetration. I was impressed. Perhaps my thoughts of the free puppy were premature.

I walked into the impressively large office with shiny marble floors and marble walls, and through the front gate to be checked by security. I noticed the security guards wearing neat little earbuds with pretty green lights flashing on the side. This promotion was everywhere. I slid my card over the sensor and walked through, and several of the guards nodded to me as they always did but seemed to giggle as people walked by. I then walked to the bank of elevators in the center of the building that would take me to another floor and set me on my mundane day of little and nothingness. Such is the life of an amazing IT professional.

The elevator was fast, as always, and as I went up to the 23rd floor, I noticed numerous green lights beside me. There certainly was a plethora of earbuds, thanks to the promotion. I wish I had thought of it. A little promotion like this will make millions of dollars for somebody. In fact, you could probably take over the world by giving away something free that had a catch.

On the 23rd floor, I walked out to an office full of craziness. My job was to help a group of programmers effectively manage their code. Nowadays, people called it DevOps, but it has been called many things. Effectively, I had to wrangle people, get code put together for releases, and meet the company's timelines. No pressure there, huh?

Three different programmers ran up to me as I walked off the elevator and told me the latest release was bad. I looked at them side-eyed and said, "We checked this last night when it went out. What has changed?"

They looked at each other and then at me. Jim Canyon spoke first, "Nobody is working on anything."

"Does that mean the code is bad or is something else going on?" I asked.

"Nobody is on the site, nobody is communicating, and we've had no support calls," Jim said. "The code must be bad, or someone would have been calling."

I walked to my desk and set my satchel down. I walked into the conference room behind my desk and motioned for them to follow. "Let's work the problem."

The four of us sat in front of the big computer in the conference room and pulled up our site. The site appeared rapidly, with numerous products flashing across the top screen and several specials in the ribbon. I clicked on one of the new office features. The item updated as it was supposed to. I checked, and nothing was wrong. I then went to the dashboard and used the special code for testing, which worked flawlessly.

"So, what is wrong?" I asked.

Jim reached over my shoulder and tapped a few keys. A dashboard appeared and showed zero users online.

"Is the network online?" I was using my troubleshooting voice.

"Duh, first thing we checked," Sarah Hawkins rolled her eyes at me.

"Okay," I was confused. "Have we checked any other sites?"

Jim tapped a few more keys, and they showed numerous sites owned by our company. A few sites showed one and two people, and one of the gaming sites showed thousands, but most of them were zeros.

"Has anyone checked the Internet?" I was still a little perplexed at this time.

"The Internet is fine," Brad Martin quipped. "Everything is fine except there are no people working in our building or any of the buildings here in town."

I looked outside the conference room window for a moment at all the people and wondered what could keep everyone off of the Internet? Even more important, what would keep everyone from buying from our site, one of the top sites in the country? As I watched out the window, I saw little green lights walking around the hallways aimlessly. The little green lights attached to the earbuds that had been given to anyone who wanted them. I looked at the four other people with me. Then I looked out the window again for just a moment.

"Did any of you get these free earbuds?"

"Yeah, I got a pair. I haven't tried them yet. Can't imagine they're anywhere close to my gaming headset. I'll probably give them to the kids."

I looked back at the screen, and there was no movement, nothing going on. I was a little beside myself because I didn't want to recompile the entire site and bring it down. Especially not if everything was working. I walked out of the conference room for a second and over to Jennifer Leary, an admin assistant that was working on the project. I asked her to join us in the conference room. As we walked into the room, she giggled a little. I looked at her, curious as to what was funny.

"Jennifer," I directed, "can you please sit down and show us the new features we rolled out?"

"I don't really need anything, thank you," Jennifer giggled again.

"I understand that, but can you help us out?" I implored.

"I'm sorry," Jennifer was giggling, "I don't think I can help you." With that she got up and left the room.

"Well, that was crazy," Sarah laughed. "I think she needs to check into the looney bin."

I watched outside through the open door that Jennifer had left dangling. I walked out and over to the interns. "Can any of you help us for a moment with testing?"

All of them looked up at me like I was crazy, "No." It was a very direct word and a very easy answer. The six interns started giggling at each other and listening to who knows what on their earbuds.

I scanned the floor, and almost everyone wasn't doing much of anything. As I watched, there were people walking back and forth down the hallway with no real intent. The interns were pecking at their keyboards and giggling hysterically, but there was nothing being typed, and no work being done. Even the scrum masters and product owners were just standing in a corner together, almost as though they were playing "Ring Around the Rosie." There was no rhyme or reason to it.

I walked back into the conference room and closed the door. Something weird was going on.

"There's something very strange going on right now," I was a little antsy. "No one out there is willing to help, and they all seem to be lost in whatever is playing on those earbuds."

"Well, let's see what's playing," Sarah reached into her pocket and pulled out a set. She opened the box carefully, and the ear pods resembled any headphones you would have gotten from a major manufacturer. She put them on the table and looked at me. "Got a knife?"

I handed her my knife, and she pried the earbud open at the side. There was a plastic coating over the inside wiring, and as she peeled it back all hell broke loose. A bug the size of a fingernail jumped out and attached itself to her finger. Sarah jumped in shock and screamed as we saw a little bit of blood come from her finger. The rest of us moved to help but she was much quicker and took my knife and cut the small insect in half. The front half was still moving as she used the knife blade to scrape it away from her and then took a glass from the center of the table and covered the two pieces of the still skittering insect.

"What the fuck is that?" I asked.

"Whatever it is, it sure wanted to get inside of my finger." Sarah took a napkin from the table and blotted the small spot on her hand. "I can't imagine what would have happened if I had put the damn things in my ears."

I looked out our conference room window and was now wondering how many of these people were being eaten alive from the inside. I stood up and walked out for a moment. There was a small supply cabinet across from my desk, and I walked to that supply cabinet. Inside were numerous displays, and among them, a small head for displaying sunglasses and jewelry. I took it out while carefully watching the rest of the area. Most people were just giggling, but some were just staring at the wall now. I walked back into the conference room. I put the head and bust on the table and picked up the second earbud. I put it to the ear of the bust and pressed the button. Moments later, there was scratching as the earbud flashed red. Then I heard the scratching get deeper, and the earbud turned green. The scratching appeared to get frantic. It was as though whatever was released from the earbud was searching inside of the head bust. It was only a matter of moments later that I saw the eye of the bust start to slowly peel aside as something inside was scratching its way out. The bug we had just seen had a twin and it was coming out to visit. Picking up my knife again, I stabbed it as it came out the eye and it struggled in pain. I pulled it out and set it on the table by jamming my knife into the table.

The four of us looked out of the conference room to all the people and the green ear pods they were wearing. All of those people, all of those bugs, what were they doing to their brains?

"Alright, I think we're inside of a new episode of night of the living zombie dead people or at least night of the living brainless interns, what do we do?" Brad was looking at each of us in turn as he spoke.

"Don't look at me Brad, I'm the helpless woman who's probably going to die. If this was a horror movie I've already been bit by the bug and it's going to slowly take over." Even in a situation like this Sarah was snarky.

"Do we think it's safe to leave? Do we think it's safe to still be here?" Jim was asking the right questions.

"I don't think we're in any direct danger." I wasn't really sure, but it sounded good. "it's more likely that whatever is going on inside of their heads it's making them more malleable. Think about how Jennifer acted. She just didn't care, and her brain is probably being eaten out very slowly. Anyone wanna guess how long it would take a bug that size to eat an entire brain or at least to eat to a point where the host died?"

"That's kind of a silly question. You're assuming that this bug knows the difference between different parts of the brain. If it does, we can expect to see different behavior. If it doesn't, we can expect to see people start dropping."

"Well now we have our expert," I laughed. "I guess that Martin is going to get us out of here."

"I doubt it," Martin was sullen. "I think I'm with Sarah. I'll probably be the first one to die."

"Well, I think I'm going to try to go home." I was thinking that would be a first step with the second step being heading to the country. The land of pesticides and good old boys with large weapons. "I'm going to get my car and head to my grandfather's house. He doesn't have Internet, or a cell phone and these earbuds would be useless to him. I would say this is a city phenomenon for now. If you guys want to go with me, let's go."

The three looked at each other and stood up even before I did. "You're not going anywhere without us."

"What about our jobs, guys?" Jim asked.

"I'm more worried about us surviving right now. If you want to stay and monitor zero sales with our exciting interns and staff, go ahead." I was a little pointed but trying to be realistic. "If we find somebody or a group that haven't put these damn things in, we will bring them or go wherever."

"What about the news?" Sarah was looking on her phone, "I can't find anything about these ear pods or about anything going on right now. Don't you think somebody else would have noticed by now?"

"Maybe we're right at the start, but you're right. Have you tried any of the news stations here in town?" I asked.

Martin and Jim were already on their phones. I was used to this. If I pointed out a problem this team would immediately dive on it and try to come up with a solution. They were good on their own, but it didn't take much if they were directed to make them into great.

"Look at this," Martin had found something and pointed his phone at us all. The large screen on the plus sized phone made it easy to see the two newscasters with their green ear pods, giggling and laughing, and not reporting news at all. As we watched, we saw several technicians run to them and try to figure out what was wrong. As we watched, the screens went dark and then a test pattern came up.

"If you like that, check this out." Jim showed his phone, and it was a very popular morning show where pure chaos had erupted. On the floor you could see a man with his head partially missing and crawling all over the floor were numerous bugs like the ones we just killed. It was a scene out of a horror movie or a very bad nightmare. As we watched, one of the cameramen fell to the ground and his face was covered by bugs in seconds, only to have them scatter away as he started giggling. "Bet a few got in that noggin," Jim chuckled.

"I'm glad you think this is funny," Sarah was suddenly serious. "This pretty much means we've got to get out of here before these guys start exploding. Either that, or we need to find some very big cans of Raid."

"We don't even know if it would do anything." I was direct, "We would be better off using force than waiting for a chemical to take effect."

Jim was glued to his phone watching the black bugs scurry across the floor and attack people on the set of the news show. "I wish I had some popcorn." He leaned back.

"I don't think we're taking this seriously enough," I said, and Jim put down his phone. "We could have a bunch of exploding bug factories at any time. We need to get out of here somehow. At minimum, we need to find a safe place. I still think the country is the best option, and I'm leaving right now. That last feed has pretty much sold me to being away from anyone that has these things in them."

I got up and moved to the door and watched the chaos outside. People were throwing things at each other and generally out of control. A man and a woman from HR were naked on one of the desks having sex as other men joined. The woman was laughing and screaming. I think her name was Penelope, and I had never seen her without a turtleneck on. Now she was definitely not shy. I moved towards the elevator and the intern, Jennifer, saw me. She started taking off her clothes and looking at me with more than the giggly abandon she had earlier. I changed course and went through a row of cubicles for the stairs. Jennifer was following until Sam, one of our testers walked up to her with only his shoes on. She stopped paying attention to me as Sam picked her up and slammed her on to the nearest desk. They both squealed in delight as I opened the stairwell door.

Thankfully, the stairs were empty. The four of us made our way down one flight at a time. On each floor, we heard screaming and laughing. On several floors, we would peek out and see the chaos. It was looking really bad. Above us, we suddenly heard a noise and looked up. A group was coming down from the upper floors.

"Who's down there?" we heard one of them say.

"It's Tim from the 23rd floor," I replied as the others moved down slowly behind me.

"Okay, Tim from the 23rd floor, do you have any idea what's going on?"

"We think so," I replied. "We are pretty sure it is directly tied to the earbuds that were being given out, free. They appear to be a triggering device to release a small bug. That bug is apparently burrowing into people's brains and making them into psychopaths or at least releasing all of their inhibitions."

"That makes sense," the voice said as it came around on the platform we were on. It was John McCain. He was the president of the company and had several of his board members with him. "We were in a board meeting when my assistant went a little crazy. She was wearing those ear pods and being more than a little inappropriate."

"That's an understatement," a woman I didn't know said from behind him. "We're trying to get out of here. Every floor seems to be the same."

"We saw part of a newscast where one of the victims' heads exploded and the entire room was covered with the little bugs. They appeared to attack everyone in range. We're trying to get out of here and head to the country." Jim looked at his phone again. "Now that station is a test pattern, as well."

"We were thinking we would go to one of our houses and hold up." John was moving past us with his group of six. "Let us know how you do."

We stood and waited while they moved down several levels. "Well, it was nice to meet the boss in the stairwell." We continued our descent and could hear them below us, working their way down to the ground floor. At about the 10th floor we heard a commotion and looked through the center of the stairwell. The floor was moving, well not exactly moving. I saw our company president running up the stairs with only a few of his people behind him. A moment later we saw him trip and be overcome by hundreds of hungry bugs.

"I think it's time we change stairwells or go higher," Sarah said as she tried the door on the tenth floor.

At this point I was wondering if there was any way to get out of the building. Certainly, there wouldn't be now. As I looked down the stairwell the floor moved in an eerie pattern, and I knew the other stairwell would likely be no better. "Let's try each of the doors and get any food on each floor and work our way to the top floor. I doubt there's any way we're going to get to the bottom right now and if we can hold out for the rest of the day, and maybe through tomorrow, maybe the world will have changed a little. Maybe somebody can fix this."

"We should work our way up and start at the 15th so at least we have a little distance between us and this black wave coming up the stairs." Martin was going up the stairs and looking down as he climbed each step. I expected him to trip and fall as he was not paying attention to where he was going but when he got to the landing he stopped and continued around the corner to go higher.

We worked our way to the 15th floor and then tried the door. It opened easily. "Martin you and Jim check this floor and then meet us at the landing of the 16th. Sarah and I will try the 16th floor. Look for any type of food, open any refrigerators, and if anybody is normal bring them along. We're gonna need all the help we can get."

Sarah and I worked our way up the stairs to the 16th floor and entered the door easily. It was part of our company, so we scanned our badges and got in. It was almost chaos as people were dancing and generally being very strange. It looked like no one's head had exploded yet and there were no bugs to be found. We went immediately to the refrigerator in the break room and there were at least six lunches. I found a box next to the refrigerator as Sarah silently took all of the food and put it in the box. We worked our way back and saw another break room with a snack machine inside. No one was in the break room and Sarah closed the door. "I'll just make short work of this." She pulled out a paper clip and started to work on the lock. I thought about the time.

"Step back for a second." I picked up a chair and Sarah stepped out of the way as I smashed the plastic keeping the snacks from us. It broke easily and we carefully reached in and pulled everything out. Our box was now overflowing but it didn't matter. We were off to the next floor.

We weren't challenged all the way back to the stairwell and as we walked into the stairwell, Jim and Martin were waiting. "Nothing in there," Martin was looking down the stairwell watching the whispering creatures make their way up the stairs. "It looks like you guys hit paydirt. Fifteen was locked up tight."

We went up to the 17th floor landing and again split up. Jim and Martin began walking into 17 as Sarah and I started walking up the stairs, but they slammed the door immediately and followed us. Jim's voice was high as he said, "Wrong floor, we need to go up a few more. That one looks a little bit over-occupied with little black scurrying critters."

We went all the way to the 20th floor and as we opened that door again, it was assailed by hundreds of little black creatures.

We decided we were going to have to work with what we had and went all the way up to the 25th floor. We were hoping that since that floor was for executives and wasted a significant amount of space, that we would not have to worry about any bugs or strange psychotic people currently having their brains eaten by an ear pod induced creature. The 25th floor was clear. The lights were on, but no one was home. There was a lock on the door, as well, on this floor. None of the other doors had locks. Working as a team we went to the two stairwells and stuffed the bottom with anything we could find until they were jammed shut. Our issue now was the ventilation system. I severely doubted that we could keep anything out for long given the huge ventilation shafts, but we found a conference room that only had two vents and they were floor vents instead of the wide ceiling vents. We stuffed those closed and move the table around so we could watch the door area. We didn't want to suffocate ourselves, so we left the door open initially.

"Let's bring the refrigerator in here," I said, and we worked our way to the 25th floor break room. There were three giant refrigerators full of food. It looks like this is where they kept the food for events, and we had no way of moving a refrigerator that large. We tried and were able to move one into the middle of the floor, but it was a lot of work. With patience we worked together and got that single refrigerator into the boardroom. Martin, Jim, and I were sweating hard. We plugged the refrigerator in and checked it realizing we had just moved a refrigerator full of water and drinks and could have made our job a lot easier if we would have unloaded it first.

We went back to the kitchen and emptied the other refrigerators then changed things around so the perishable items would stay cold and things like water and soda could get warm. Martin got a computer and was able to log on very rapidly. We started watching different streams and saw that the city was in chaos. It appeared that this event was limited to our city, but the news was now out to not accept anything that could be put in your ear.

Hours passed and we wondered how everything was going to work out. We were all tense and the constant scratching in the stairs had not helped. It was then that we started to see the army on streams. People knew what was happening now and a small group of scientists showed the progression on a streaming channel of how the bug was activated and then bred and destroyed its host. It was very gruesome, but I think some people needed to see it.

To make matters worse, a tic toc challenge came out to try to see how long you could wear them and not get infected. The net was filled with videos of stupid people screaming in pain as they tried to wrench out the headphones.

Martin was pacing like there was no tomorrow. "I am tired of this, maybe they are gone." He walked to the door and listened, then walked back to the open conference room door. "I can't hear them anymore."

175

"We have to hold on, you saw the videos, it is crazy out there." I was trying to lead, but the situation was out of control.

"Martin is right," Jim echoed. "We could be out of here and not in danger if we just left now. We don't know how long these things can even live."

"Guys let's stick together," Sarah was obviously scared now. The videos of the challenges had made her lose her faith in humanity.

I started pacing with them. "We can't just try to go out. We don't know what's behind the doors."

"What do you want us to do? Stay up here and when they come up here, go up to the roof then jump? I'd rather take my chances going down the stairs." Martin was turning red.

"Look at this video," Sarah was looking at her phone. "It says we're on the edge of the infection area. The army is here using flamethrowers on everything. Maybe this building is clear now."

"Well, I'm going to find out," Martin said and walked to the door.

"Martin don't do it," I was backing up towards the conference room.

Martin opened the door, and the 1-foot layer of black bugs began to roll into the room. Martin fell backwards and screamed as he was engulfed by the slithering mass. I was back in the conference room and turned to see Jim falling under the mass as well. His hand reached out and then was gone.

Sarah slid into the room as I slammed the door. I jammed our makeshift stops underneath it, and closed everything up including the vents in the floor.

It wasn't much longer before we heard scratching at the door. I took the small table to the side and pressed it against the bottom of the door as well and moved another small file cabinet against it.

Sarah was crying. She was kicking her legs constantly on the floor and smacking herself in the face it's just saying, "No, no, no." I went to her, and she screamed when I touched her shoulder. I didn't know what to do so I slapped her, and she sobbed and looked at me holding her cheek.

"You're not helping."

"Jim and Martin," Sarah began.

"They're dead because they decided that they knew better. You're alive because you were at least cautious. We can stay here until the army clears this building. I can't have you out of control. I'm gonna need your help to watch and make sure none of those things get in here."

Sarah blubbered for a few more seconds, then stopped and said, "Okay."

I recorded a video as quickly as I could, "I'm sure I won't be able to remember this story for long; the world seems to be a miasmic shroud of what it used to be. If the door doesn't hold, I will soon be part of the mindless. I give this to you as a warning, but perhaps there is no one left." I saved it and it went to the cloud and on my social media account. Perhaps somebody would see some good out of it.

Sarah seemed to be more alert and began watching the area. We watched all around and I looked out the window on the door and saw all of the floor covered. She got on her phone and looked at the fires being started burning away the bugs. They were in our building.

"It's probably why they're being forced up here." I watched the video over her shoulder. "As they clear the floors more and more are gonna run up here, we just have to survive.

Sarah stared as the live cameras started showing as the flamethrowers burned people and bugs alike. It looked like a scene out of hell or worse than hell, Sarah cried softly to herself. I looked out the window and the bugs were over three feet deep and rising. Over to the side I saw tables moving around being pushed by the sheer weight of the insects. We watched the video and saw them go up floor by floor.

"That's 23," Sarah pointed to her screen; "That was my desk." The flames now burned on the computer and the desk. A team moved into the stairwell and the camera panned down to see flames below and teams putting out the fires with extinguishers. The camera panned up and you could see thousands upon thousands of bugs running up the stairs. Flames shot out in front of the camera, and I heard strange sounds.

I could hear them outside now. The open door showed flames but then darkness closed in as the bugs covered the window. I could no longer see out of the conference room. Sarah whimpered and we could see golden light flashing but not see anything else through all of the insects. It began getting warm and I knew the fire was likely around us. I saw the flames hit the window and the window begin to melt away. There were other shots of flame and I wondered how long the glass would hold. I saw the window begin to warp and realized it wasn't glass but instead was acrylic or plastic.

"They're gonna burn us up," Sarah was whimpering.

"We're in here! We're in here," she screamed. "Don't kill us!"

I heard men outside and heard the thrush of flamethrower that we had seen on the screen minutes ago. The door rumbled.

An axe came through the door. I held Sarah close, and she clung to me whimpering. I saw a face through a helmet as the door was ripped away and two men walked in. They were dressed in silver suits, and both had flamethrowers on them. A small pilot light was lit at the front of the flamethrower and both men had thick gloves. I looked at their boots and they were covered with the carcasses of bugs, crushed and burned.

"We're okay, we're okay," Sarah was ecstatic. "We're saved."

"I saw the flames slowly spray out from one of the men's flamethrowers. It was as though it was in slow motion and the fire was alive, like some hungry beast ravenous for anything that could feed it. The flames surrounded Sarah and she danced almost like a marionette screaming as the men watched. A second later I saw the flames coming at me. I thought I was going to live but obviously that was another story.

About the Author

Andrew Allen Smith was born in Anderson, Indiana. Until the age of fifteen, he moved at least once per year and finally settled in Lexington, Kentucky. Andrew spent a significant amount of his teenage years reading and writing short stories, attempts at novels, and poetry. He published his first book, "A Slice of Passion," in 2005. It was a book of poetry compiled from dozens of years of work.

In 2015, Andrew published "The Theft and Other Short Stories" as a collection of some of his favorite portions of his writings after he was challenged to self-publish a book. Challenged and excited about his success, he published his first novel, "Vengeful Son," in 2016 and began building a franchise with that book. "The Masterson Files" (the series containing "Vengeful Son") now includes five books and has fifteen in outline form. The story follows an ex-assassin that is reluctantly engaged in helping others while trying to retire.

In 2020, after a tragic event, Andrew co-wrote "What NOT to Say to People Who Are Grieving." This book showcased emotions and an approach to helping others be more mindful of their words during grief.

2021 gave us "A Slice of Fear" followed by "Another Slice of Fear" with short stories focusing on fears of all types. "Another Slice of Fear" won Andrew a Literary Titan Award and has been reviewed positively for several stories in the genre.

As Quality Leader and System Architect, Andrew's work gave him credit for a series of instructional manuals for site relationship management systems, various quality documents, and development lifecycles. In Andrew's spare time, he has a passion for many hobbies and his family, which he considers paramount. For more information about Andrew, please visit **andrewallensmith.com**.

Books by Andrew Allen Smith

Fiction
A Slice of Passion
A Slice of Fear
Another Slice of Fear
Yet Another Slice of Fear
The Theft and Other Short Stories

The Masterson Files Series
Vengeful Son
Sinful Father
Deadly Daughter
Fateful Friend
Silent Sister

The Eternal Forever Series
Adam

Non-Fiction
What NOT to say to People Who are Grieving

Books Containing Andrew Allen Smith's prose
Monster Hunter Intern and Other Tales
The Gift and Other Stories
Simple Things: Moments of Isolated Gratitude
The Portrait of Herbert Losh and Other Stories
The Drifter and Other Unusual Tales

Coming Soon
Burial Ground
Stealth Drive
The Masterson Files Book 6 - Curious Cousin
The Eternal Forever Book 2 – Morgan
Another Slice of Passion